Crack the Spine

Spring 2013

Edited by Kerri Farrell Foley

CONTENTS

Memo Line

My head smacks against the window as I jolt awake. Mom is playing Bob Seger and my little brother is eating his shirtsleeve. The wet spot spiders out through the weave of an orange-dyed, cotton-blend tee. They named him Von, which is weird, but they held some desperate hope that by giving a sick fetus a name that means "hope" God would fix him or something. Maybe it would have helped if they actually went to church.

I was nine when she got pregnant. She was forty-five and he was an accident. I had finally gotten used to her swollen stomach and fat toes. We had just painted the nursery sky blue with little white clouds. I had gotten to help with the stencils.

When Mom came home that day she learned her oops baby would be born sick, her face was so splotched from crying that she looked discolored. Dad went pale as if he already knew what she was going to say—they had a choice to make. Mom told me to go to my room; Mommy and Daddy needed to talk. I stomped off to my room where I threw all the pillows off my bed and cried until I was red in face and fell asleep, still hiccupping for air. I was an only child until Vonny.

I was still bitter when Grandpa took me to the hospital to see Mom and the baby. The hallways were floored in glossy turquoise colored tiles and the doorknobs were shiny silver. I watched my distorted reflection change as I moved my head back and forth in front of it. Mom looked tired. Her normally straight hair was matted in waves at her forehead. Her brown eyes were glassy and swollen. I hid behind Grandpa's leg. Daddy was nowhere to be found.

"Momma?" I had asked. "Are you okay?"

She didn't smile or placate me with whispers of how everything would be okay. Instead, she stared and whispered something of a yes. She was looking straight at me, but it was wrong. Her eyes looked like the bottom of glass cups: curved and clear but diluted. Vonny looked weird too. His head was too big and his face was wide. His round blue eyes almost looked in different directions and his nose was flat. He didn't look like Mom or Dad. When they brought him in no one smiled. Mom cried and held him like spoiled little white girls hold black baby dolls—as if he was strange, foreign.

They took him away quickly. I guess his heart was broken too. Grandpa said there was a hole and that they sewed it together with a needle and thread. I played with my Cabbage Patch Doll, Tabitha, on the blue speckled carpet of the waiting room. Vonny tore her arm last year in a manic fit. I still haven't forgiven him.

He's mumbling something while still chewing through his Bob the Builder shirt. His puffed belly peeks out and I can just see where his belly button hides amidst a roll of fat. He looks at me with wild, round doe eyes.

"What do you need?" I ask with an exaggerated *eed*. I'm trying to tune out Seger with Sigur Ros, but my headphones are the cheap kind that Mom probably bought at Rite Aid the day before she stuffed them into my hot pink Christmas stocking. I don't even like pink anymore. After Dad left, she stopped caring about string-light covered reindeer and heart-shaped pb&j's.

"Headphones!" Vonny shouts.

Mom's sigh sounds more like a wheeze. She barely dodges a hacking smoker's coughing fit before saying, "What do you say, Von?"

"Please. Headphones!" he shrieks, already impatient. He kicks his sausage legs against his booster seat and pounds a fist against his leg. He pauses for a moment to examine the pink splotch forming near his knee.

The wild eyes are back. They're so glossy that they're reflective. My head looks too skinny in his round eyes. "Head. Phones!" he squeals in single syllables, this time reaching out a fat dimpled hand. He's five but refuses to use real sentences. I'm starting to think he's lazy.

"No, I'm listening to music. Eat your shirt."

"Kaitlin!" Mom shouts. "For God's sake, give him a break. We've only been in the car for an hour and a half." In the rear view mirror, I see her eyes narrow and the great wrinkle divide between her eyes.

"Whatever."

Bob's blasting louder on the stereo and Von is grinding his teeth. Dad never would have let me respond to her that way. He was all about manners and respect and other shit.

"What do you say?" he asked the night of my first sleepover.

"Please and thank you," I sighed, knowing the drill.

"And what do you call her mom?" he asked next.

"Ma'am and Ms.," I'd responded with already squirming feet, ready to run off to play.

"Good girl. I love you, Sweetie. Be good," he'd say before giving my shoulders a squeeze and sending me off. He and Mom had waved from the front door as I hopped into Becka's mom's car, forgetting everything he had just said.

I hear the high-pitched scraping sound of his teeth grinding together. It makes my own teeth hurt and he lets out a chuckle. He always grinds his teeth. Most of them are already covered in silver crowns. The porcelain-colored ones cost extra.

"Stop it, Von," I say. "You'll ruin your teeth."

"Will you grab his mouth guard?" Mom says. "It's in the bag. He knows he's not supposed to be doing that."

I dig through her black stretched leather bag. Cigarettes, cigarettes, sunglasses, an Ann Rice novel, an assortment of pill bottles, mouth guard. "Here, put this in your mouth," I say as I push the blue sparkly puck into his reaching hand.

He grabs it and instantly launches it toward the front seat. It's possible that he has a future career as a javelin thrower. It hits the dash and bounces off into some French fry laden crevice.

"Damnit, Kaitlin! You know that you can't just hand it to him!" she shrieks while unbuckling her seatbelt. She has one hand on the wheel and is leaning over the passenger seat with her hand down the treacherous space between the center console and the seat. The car begins to rattle as the van crawls over the yellow line. She whips the wheel back and we are in the right lane again. Some two-door coop honks and speeds past. "Shit," Mom mutters.

Vonny chuckles. "Shhit!" he mimics.

"No, Von, don't say that," Mom scolds. He grinds his teeth in response. "Kaitlin, can you look for his mouth guard please?"

I turn the music up on my iPod. Vonny is staring at me again.

"Kaitlin, I'm talking to you."

"We can get it later. I'm not his mother."

One night long after the whispers of a sick brother surfaced, when Mom was so fat her ankles turned purple and her ring no longer fit her finger, I heard her whispering to Dad on the couch. "I don't think I can do this. I don't think I can be a good mother to him," she said. They thought that I was asleep. I saw Dad reach a hand toward her bloated belly. "I can't do this on my own," she had whispered.

"You're not alone," Dad replied. He continued on about Grandpa and how I was getting older and would be able to help. I don't want to help, I had thought. "It will be fine. Don't worry."

I don't know what happened when they finally brought Vonny home from the hospital. I stayed with Grandpa for a couple of weeks so Mom and Dad could, "get the baby settled."

"You don't want me at home?" I had said to my mother in the hospital before leaving with Grandpa.

She was all cried out. "Kaitlin, you know that isn't true. Your brother is sick and we need to get settled at home."

"But I can help!" I said as I stamped my foot. "I want to help."

Vonny is still grinding his teeth. Now he's playing with the automatic window switch. Mom has the lock on so he can't roll the window down and lose a limb or something. I close my eyes and try to sleep. I hear the dull scraping sound of Von's teeth as I doze off.

"Okay guys, this week we are studying brain disorders," my biology teacher had announced a few weeks ago. Great, Vonny's following me to school now. "We are going to be looking at chromosomal disorders first. The most well known of these is Down's Syndrome," he said. "And if I were you, I'd take notes. I have a feeling this might show up on the exam next week." The class groaned but I learned that my brother has an extra chromosome. Awesome.

That was the same week Janette in my English class asked me to hang out. With her bushel of brown curls she leaned over and said, "We should have a sleepover."

"Sure, that'd be fun," I replied.

"The only thing is, I don't have my own room."

I paused. It was my turn to speak. Her oval face lay open, inviting. "Oh, that sucks." I didn't know what else to say. It's not like I could invite her over with Von screaming and Mom crying.

Her penciled brows lowered and she looked away toward the pearlescent glow of the white board. The room smelled strongly of marker. I felt sick.

When I finally got to come back home, the change that came with Vonny's arrival was tangible. There were bottles everywhere and a woman with a thick brown braid and an Indian accent would come every day to try to get Vonny to drink Mom's milk. One day I asked why I didn't get her milk too. Mom looked disgusted. "That is only for babies, Kaitlin. You need to be a big girl now," she said as if each word was a sprint and she was out of breath. I was embarrassed. I didn't understand why he got all her attention. Apparently neither did Dad.

It seemed like he got home later and later each night. Sometimes it was just in time to kiss me goodnight. "Can you just hold him for a second?" Mom would ask as she placed Vonny, wild-eyed and squirming, into his arms. He would stare down at him like a spooked horse. He held him tight but didn't really look at him.

There were doctor appointments, tons of them. Mom no longer had time to braid my hair in the morning. Vonny was always sick. They said he was a colicky baby. All I knew was that mom bought me earplugs to drown out his late-night screams.

But there was always something wrong. I'd stare at his wide face and toothless smile while trying to force mushed-up bananas down his throat. I didn't dare have friends over. When they did come over they didn't coo and coddle him like they did other babies. They were silent, twiddling their thumbs, and wondering what was wrong with Kaitlin's little brother. They wondered if I had it too.

"Stop it, Vonny!" I groan. He's playing with the door handle now. Pulling the plastic arm back and forth, back and forth. Mom has some special lock on it she has to lock every time we get in the car.

"I need to smoke," Mom sighs from the front. "I'm sure Von needs to pee. Are you hungry?"

I'm always hungry, I think, but stopping means that we have to unpack Von, which takes forever. We stop at the Del Taco. There is a large purple sign advertising forty-nine cent burritos. There's a couple my age groping each other on the sidewalk and sharing a soda. They stop to watch us enter. Vonny holds onto Mom's shrunken t-shirt and resumes chewing his own.

"One thing each," Mom says as she stuffs a few dollar bills into my hand. "I'll be outside." I see her reach into her jacket pocket for her lighter. She didn't smoke until Dad left. Every time we'd walk by a smoker he'd say something like "Think about how gross her lungs must be," or "Did you smell that?" Since then I've wondered if Mom had always craved cigarettes or if she just took them up because Dad hated them.

I also don't remember worrying about money until Vonny. Doctor's appointments, therapy sessions, dentist appointments, cardiologist appointments—they all cost money. Dad's gone so Mom is left paying all the bills. He sends a check a month with the words, "CHILD SUPPORT" spelt out in all-caps chicken scratch in the memo line. It comes in a generic white envelope, often with a sticky note as a letter. Things like, "I miss you, Kiddo," or "Hope you guys didn't get hit too hard by the storm." I couldn't give two shits about the storm.

The Del Taco smells like burnt beans and dirty hands. I reach over and grab Vonny's clammy hand. He wriggles free from my grasp. "Stop touching that," I snap. Vonny's playing with the edge of the plastic table. It has a Spanish-inspired design that Del Taco apparently interpreted into red, green, and yellow zigzags. Mom walks back in and asks if we ordered. I tell her no and that I was too busy watching her child. She grabs the crumpled bills out of my hand and growls, "Sit down."

There is a family sitting in the opposite corner near the burrito sign. A little girl in overalls meets my gaze and gives me a nervous smile.

"Don't stare. It's rude," I hear her mother whisper. The other little girl is completely enraptured by the video game she has hidden under the table. The father squeezes the mother's shoulder as she looks at him with a tense frown. He looks at me with a slight shrug, almost apologetic. Yeah, I know you're sorry he's my brother, or maybe just happy that he isn't your son.

I hear a jagged inhale and a faint whine. Vonny is staring at his finger. I see a small drop of blood welling up near his index finger's cuticle. There is a smear of his red DNA on the ragged edge where he ripped up some of the plastic table corner.

"Jesus, Von!" I say. He starts breathing quickly and whining louder. I see the flicker of panic in his crystal blue eyes. He's crying now. I fight with the metal napkin dispenser and rip them all as I attempt to extricate a few. "Shh, here. Take these," I say as I shove the handful of crumpled napkins toward his hand. He hits them out of my hand and they scatter over the floor like big, ugly confetti.

He's screaming now and sounds like one of the baby chimps on the Discovery Channel. Mom walks toward us. "What is going on?" she says through gritted teeth, her cheeks already colored a flaming red hue. "What did you do?" she snaps at me before bending down to try to placate Vonny.

We're a circus, a show. A too-thin mother wishing she had another cigarette clenched between her teeth, an ungrateful daughter wanting a second of her mother's time, and a five-year-old boy with Downs, running amuck, being blamed for it all. And everyone is staring.

The family in the corner is no longer concerned with being rude. An elderly couple two plastic booths down are subtly shaking their heads in disapproval. When they reach their thirteen-year-old Buick they will say things like, "People like that shouldn't have children" and "Where is that child's father? All he needs is a good spanking."

His crying has turned into screeching. It's the kind of sound that you imagine Velociraptors made during challenging births. But then you realize that they laid eggs and reconsider how painful that process really was. Mom has her purse on her shoulder again and is trying to shush Vonny. She's whispering empty threats into his ear now, offering him candy, and then eventually pleading with him. It's futile. His screams echo against the plastic green fauna and low foam tiled ceiling. The man at the cash register is looking directly at us. A woman at the middle table stuffs her burrito into her bag and gets up. "You should probably go through the drive-thru next time," she says with fake smile that looks more like a cringe. I think of the bean and cheese burrito smelling up her purse.

"Mom, can we please go?" I almost cry.

"What do you think I'm trying to do? Just be quiet!" she half shrieks and half whispers. "Vonny, we need to go," she says tugging at his arm. He starts to thrash and scream louder. "God damnit, Kaitlin! Help me." We are, what my friend Danielle calls, a shit show.

I grab one arm that flails wildly as if it is some boneless tentacle. We drag him out and he continues to scream. His face is bright red and someone claps as we exit. I let go when we are almost to the car.

"Kailtin!" Mom screams while trying to calm Von down. "You can't help me for one fucking second?"

"I'm not the one having a meltdown! We can't even eat lunch with him," I yell back. "He's so embarrassing." And before I can stop it, it floods out, "Dad would never have let this happen."

Mom's face turns pale. She looks away and tries again to quiet Von. She finally just grabs him around his belly and heads toward the car. "Just get in the car, Kaitlin," she says without looking my way. Von is still screaming. I think of Dad the night before he left. Vonny had thrown a terrible tantrum and couldn't be calmed. The house looked like a tornado had displaced dirty towels and broken toys in our living room. "You take care of him for once," Mom had just yelled before storming out the front door with keys in hand.

Dad just sat on the couch and stared as his three-year-old son writhing on the carpet, screaming so hard he could barely breathe. He was crouched over and staring at his hands. He twisted his wedding band round and round. When Mom came back, Vonny had already cried himself to sleep. He was face down on the carpet in a twisted fetal position. There was a small glob of green vomit next to his face. She looked from Vonny to Dad and back to Vonny. She shook her head as she pulled him gently into her arms, wiping his face. Her eyes were bloodshot and her spine showed through her shirt like marble stepping-stones.

She took Vonny to the nursery. Dad finally looked up. He walked over and wrapped his arms around me. I could feel his quick breath against my ear. "I love you, Kaitlin. Don't forget that," he said and grabbed his keys. Mom came in and scrubbed the carpet. She sprayed it with cleaner and used *Chicken Soup for the Family's Soul* as a weight atop the paper towel.

Mom's phone begins to ring as she's wrestling a still-screaming Vonny into the car seat. "Shit, I have to take this," she sighs. She holds the phone against her ear with her shoulder and pulls Vonny's arm through a strap of the car seat. I reach over to help.

"Just leave it be, Kaitlin," she snaps. "Yes, I'm here. Is there any way I can call you..." she cuts off as she slams the door and gets into the driver's seat. "Yes, I know. I mailed the check last week," she says into the phone while trying to wrangle on her own seat belt.

I lean in again to try to buckle him in. My fingers fumble to fight his fidgeting as I search for the center strap. He's squealing, "K-k-k" in place of what I assume is my name. I deflect a plump flailing hand and it he hits my eye instead.

"Vonny! That hurt!" I yell as I reach my hand up to my eye.

"No, I'm still here, sorry," Mom says. She is still trying to talk on the phone.

Vonny begins his second wind of full-fledged screams.

"What is going on?" she yells from the front.

Mom careens her neck to the right to check on Von. Her eyes flicker toward me. Her sagged, almost gaunt cheek reveals the slightest twitch.

"Just leave it, Kaitlin," she growls. "You've done enough." She clicks the gear into drive with a start while eyeing me again in the rearview mirror. She begins navigating through the maze of cement parking bricks. It reminds me Tetris except if we ram into a streetlight there isn't a play again option.

I continue to search for the strap with one hand on my eye and the other in Von's car seat. "Mom, can you please get off the phone? He's still not bucked—"

"Goddamnit!" she interrupts. "I told you to—John? John, I'm going to have to call you back." She barely dodges the drive-thru entrance and makes a hard right. I see the heat seeping off the sidewalk and the face of the overalled girl in Del Taco, pressed against the window.

I'm embarrassed. I get back into my seat. My eye is burning; I think it's scratched. I hear the sound of Vonny wriggling—the Velcro strips on his cargo shorts against the velvet cover of his car seat. I press my fist against my burning eye, trying to force away the pain. I feel the hot sting of tears run down my face. I can't see anything.

"Kaitlin!" Mom yells. "Kaitlin, what is your brother doing?"

"You just told me to leave him—" I say. My hand is still attached to my eye. I don't want her to see me cry.

The door open beep chimes like church bells in the middle of the night. "Von, no!" she screams now and the car swerves. I lift my head and look through a teared eye. Von's door swings open and with a burst of the stifling hot summer air, he's gone. He's gone.

"Von!" she screams before screeching to a halt.

Vonny is screaming near a cement parking brick, just another misplaced Tetris piece. He has a fat lip and a bloody nose, but I think he's okay. The Del Taco crowd is outside now, observing from a distance. The door-open beep is still chiming from the car and Vonny is hyperventilating. He's coughing while trying to gasp for breath. He hadn't expected the door to open. He hadn't expected to be free from his constraints. My hand is still glued to my eye. It burns.

I'm thinking of the time Mom accidentally closed the car window on my arm in the first grade. Dad had laughed afterward, but Mom looked horrified. I didn't even have a scratch, but she had tears in her eyes. "She's fine, baby," Dad had said as he stretched his hand out to rub her shoulder.

Mom is crouched over Vonny. She's crying. She looks like a child holding a broken doll. "I'm so sorry, baby. I'm so sorry," she chokes out. Vonny screams, his face is swollen red and a purple bruise is forming above his left eye. I drop my hand from my face and squat down next to him to reach my hand for his flailing leg.

"You're okay, Vonny," I coo with tears freely streaming down my cheeks. "You're okay. I'm sorry." I shake as I begin to sob, "I'm sorry. It's not your fault."

The purple burrito sign glares at us. An employee in a bright yellow polo looks as if she's contemplating calling the police, but no one approaches us. My knees burn against the hot blacktop of the parking lot. Black mascara tears are traveling down the divots of Mother's face. She clenches her jaw into a twitching half-smile and looks at me. "It's not yours either." I think of generic memo lines, Mom working at the scratched kitchen table all night, and Vonny's silver-and-gap-tooth smile when I wake him up in the morning.

Cradle Song

Ripened with sun, her bedroom is empty when the girl wakes up; a daughter body warm with the milky smell from her dream-darkened pajamas. She thinks of crying mother-words to break the space between her feet and the attic door, but she fears the cradlesong might swallow her tongue.

Her underwear thickens in plastic purses, blue and pink soils beneath the mattress, soaking the wash from t-shirts pulled and tossed in the wooden drawer's child dust. She moves with moist cheeks,

> left squeak,
>
> right squeak,
>
> left.

The girl peels from her daughter skin; the wet pink of her hand shadows dripping. Inside the attic door, she whispers.

Heat Lightning

It was the third night in a row where the thermometer rested comfortably at 103 degrees, refusing to budge even a degree or two after the sun had set. So it was the third night in a row that Jane and Abbott, two newlywed and newly unemployed college graduates, had sat awake in the heat. Tonight they even tried to have sex, hoping the afterglow would negate the heat, but after some half hearted kissing and something that would be a lie if it were called heavy petting, the couple gave up. It was just too hot.

"We should go for a drive," Abbott said.

They owned a single car between the two of them- a rusting Toyota Corolla from 1994. Nothing about the car was modern, including the hand cranked windows and the conspicuous lack of air conditioning.

"It'll be better than sweating in these bed sheets all night," Abbott said. After a pause he added: "Again."

Jane couldn't argue with that logic. They stumbled into the car and rolled down the windows. Both had to twist and contort to roll the backseat windows down since neither felt like unsticking themselves from the vinyl once they were seated.

Abbott drove. Jane rested her head on the side of the door and let the night air rush over her, turning her short hair into a tornado of chaos. She was wearing a thin tank top and every once in a while a burst of air would billow it out, revealing one pink nipple. She hadn't bothered with a bra. Abbott found it difficult to keep his eyes on the road when this happened.

They drove in silence for a while until Abbott switched on the radio and found the one station the car could recieve- AM 92.2- a local smooth jazz station. The blue notes floated over the two of them as

Abbott took the roads out of town until they were driving down dark streets.

"It's funny," Jane said. "I'm sure I know this road, but it looks so strange at night."

Abbott just nodded. He knew where they were, of course, but it felt right to pretend like he didn't.

"We could be anywhere," Jane said.

The road around them seemed like it was blanketed, that she and Abbott were travelling through a tunnel to an unknown world.

"Do you hear that?" Abbott asked after some minutes of jazz.

"What?"

Abbott slowed the car. "Listen."

There seemed to be a *tch-tch* sound coming from just up ahead along the dark road. The car crawled to a stop and Jane felt the cool drops before she realized what they were from.

"It's a sprinkler."

Abbott barely took the time to kill the engine before they were both out of the car. They walked barefoot across the cool lawn and held their arms open as the droplets coated their faces and clothing.

"We look like Jesus," Abbott whispered and Jane let out a squeal. She dropped to her knees and rolled in the wet grass, before resting on her stomach, her face buried in the ground. Abbott joined her., and breathed the wet earth in.

Around them the sticky air remained, and before too long they climbed back in the car and continued to drive. The breeze felt much better on wet skin, but soon enough they were dry again and it felt like their windows were opening into an oven. Abbott made the decision to head back to their apartment.

"What was that?" Jane asked and sat upright in her seat. She craned her neck out the window as they drove.

"Hear another sprinkler?"

"No, I saw something. There!"

Abbott pulled the car over and followed her pointing finger to just above a ridge lined with trees.

"I don't see any--"

The clouds lit up.

"Fireworks?" Jane asked.

"At 3 AM?"

"Maybe some other people who couldn't sleep."

Abbott turned the car and soon they made it to the road that ran across the ridge. No one else was there. He killed the engine and the couple waited in silence for a moment before the sky was lit up again- this time by a brilliant white tree whose branches stretched and broke through the clouds. Abbott had to blink a couple of times to clear the after-image from his vision.

"What was that?" Jane whispered.

"Heat lightning." Abbott said, whispering as quietly as his wife. "We used to see it all the time when we were kids and playing in the back yard at night when it was too hot to sleep."

"So it's going to rain soon, right? Maybe that'll kill this heatwave."

"No, heat lightning doesn't mean there's a thunderstorm coming. It's kind of like a cosmic joke. All the signs of rain, but absolutely none to speak of."

"Well that's just shi-"

The sky lit up again. No thunder followed, just strike after strike of lightning that wove spider webs through the clouds. They sat in silence for a while and watched the sky. Abbott held Jane's hand and she kissed him on the cheek. Soon enough they couldn't focus on the sky and Abbott drove home quickly while his wife whispered in his ear things that shouldn't be repeated on paper.

That night they had the best sleep of their lives and the next night the heatwave broke.

And They Pretend They Can't

And they pretend they can't

read the highways.

They say they never heard the story

about a man with no arms

and a man with ghosts for arms

who fought hard and long ago.

They say they don't see

how those men twist the highways still.

Framed Beside Her
An Essay

Funny... *not* so funny... how my father, always the evangelical atheist, never mentioned that someday down the line, when I truly needed a spot of faith, a few shots of tequila might have to suffice: sole diversion to the plainness of facts. When he meets my flight from Berkeley, his familiar smell of aftershave and White Owl Tips is at first oddly comforting, but straight off, with no warm-up, he says, "Those damned books. They all say to be peaceful, but what the hell good is that right now? I hope you'll encourage her to fight this thing." Then he adds, "She's never *fought*."

"...Rage, rage, against the dying of the light."

"Damn right."

"When she can't take a full breath?"

"Ah, hell," he says, as if I'm refusing to grant him even this small victory.

In the car, when he continues to hammer me with theory rather than provide me with news, I resort to an old trick I promised myself I wouldn't: to show him how I feel, I pull a paperback from my jacket pocket and, right there next to him, casually begin to read. Kundera's *The Unbearable Lightness of Being*, which I'm reading for lit class back at UC. My father slows down for a green light, recognizes his error and over-accelerates. Beyond the firm lettering of the book, I can feel his frustration, hear him mumble to himself, "Tell your brain... tell your brain!"

At home, Mom sits propped up and blanketed in her recliner next to the blinking Christmas tree, hands folded in her lap, dozing but clearly waiting for me. Framed on the shelf beside her is a pair of old Polaroids from Martha's Vineyard: she carrying me across the beach, then the two of us in the shallow water, she, arm curled around my hip, smiling down at me as I stare off camera. Despite all the preparation from my sister, Natalie, I'm not set for the way she looks, her hair bone white, her cheeks drastically thinned, mostly loosened skin. I kiss her dry lips and she awakens. Her eyes seem larger than I've ever seen them. For a long moment she doesn't seem to know me. Then she says, "Honey. Help me to the kitchen, where the light is better."

"Sure, Mom," I say. Playfully, I place my frayed Mets cap backwards on her head, but maybe this is to ease the sight of her hair. I flip down the lever on the recliner, lift her. Distended belly, lifeless arms, tangled oxygen tube dangling from her shoulder, she is not the package that I expect; there isn't enough to hold onto. She slips through my hands like a sinker.

"Ma—I'm so sorry!" I say, as I scoop her up, notice the fresh rug burn on her elbow.

"No. It's me." She looks up at me. "I'm a mess."

We settle into an attempt at normalcy, Natalie buzzing around like an inept bee, busy with newfound chores, Dad downstairs drinking gin and pounding away at the typewriter ("Dialectics for Teenagers"), as I lie on the living room floor propped up on an elbow, reading of *Kilost*: a Polish term meaning, as far as I can understand, *humor in the midst of great suffering,* a sensibility that Kundera accuses the pubescent United States of not knowing.

For the first time since I've been home—lone, jarring proof of an outside world—the phone rings. To my surprise, Mom struggles awake and answers it. The conversation is cryptic, over quickly.

"Who was that, Mom?" Natalie calls out. Natalie, unlike me, has taken a leave of absence from college to deal with the crisis.

"Oh… nobody. Wrong number. Some pizzeria."

It is amazing here, the gnaw of dullness, the immensity of what's at stake, pages that take hours to read, hours that slip past without identity. Beyond the sliding glass doors the dogs play as normal. When the phone finally rings again, Mom is deep in troubled sleep.

"Where is she?" asks a strong male voice, as soon as I've said hello.

"Where is who?"

"*Marianne*. Why hasn't she been checked-in yet? Yesterday's blood panel... this isn't something we can play around with."

"Who *is* this?"

"Dr. Green. Didn't my nurse inform someone there that she needed to be brought in?"

"I don't think so," I say, drawing a few pieces together. "But we'll be right there."

Gently, then more firmly, I jiggle Mom awake. "Mom, was that Dr. Green's office that called earlier?"

Mom's eyes open slowly, groggy and feverish, then quickly become pensive as a disobedient child's. "It's Christmas Eve—the hospital isn't even open," she informs me.

I start to laugh, and in this small chasm, the situation suddenly becomes exponentially funnier, I can't seem to stop, I am wiping my eyes. "Natalie!" I call out, sounding the alarm. Then, more to myself, more of a nervous humm, "I'll pack a bag."

"No—no bag!" says Mom. "I don't have the right kind."

With her body swimming in its own toxins, it is impossible to gauge the level of thought beneath her duplicity, but I am struck by the immediacy of her fear: that if she is handed over to nurses, she'll never again see home, that if she is hooked up to machines, she'll never get off them.

I look on as she takes clearer measure of the situation. "I can't remember where I hid the presents I got on eBay."

"You'll remember, Mom."

"If you only hadn't picked up that phone!" she scolds me.

Kilost?

At the hospital, her blood pressure is even higher than Dr. Green feared. She is rolled immediately to ICU, hooked up to monitors and intravenous. Another hour and she would have slipped into a coma, they tell us.

Everything is left exactly in place beneath the tree. Christmas is postponed until New Year's. And Mom *does* break from the grip of those machines. Dr. Green agrees that she should be home where she wants to be. She's doing "Okay" he tells us. But late that night, her first at home, Natalie and I are awoken by cries. "Help me! Why won't you help me?"

My father, who sleeps downstairs, doesn't hear, which is probably for the best. Natalie and I arrive at Mom's bedside simultaneously. Mom is pawing at her blankets, at her pillows, in a desperate attempt to raise herself.

"Mom, calm down. You need to stay calm. It will all be okay..." It is difficult to tell who is speaking, me or Natalie.

Mom's eyes come open in slits, then wider still, as if she needs to say something of utmost importance, but can't. Natalie and I measure each other, and each take one of her hands. Mom stares at the ceiling, a great, incomprehensible void, before her eyes slip closed and stay that way.

"Mom, its okay," I whisper, "...it's okay to *let go*." I can't believe I am saying these words, have no idea if she hears them.

Her face relaxes, then her arms and legs. Natalie and I look on helplessly as Mom's breathing slows then disappears. From deep inside comes a chilling gurgle.

Uselessly, I whisper again, "Mom... it's *okay*."

Then her eyes come open again. "Why do you keep saying that? I *know* it's okay. If you would help me fluff the darn pillow!"

The next morning, when we lift her into her recliner, Mom's eyes are sharper, the hospital stay seems to have been good for her. "Why don't we go ahead and get rid of all these stacks of newspapers?" she asks. As far back as I can remember—my entire life—I've harped at Mom to give up this hopeless game of catch-up, this backlog of NY Times, The Nation, Sunset, etc., that she believes she'll one day get to. Now, when the pile feels sacred, she finally wants to give it up. "And could I have some of that walnut ice cream. And maybe a *small* snifter of cognac?" Her voice is free of all familiar constraint. *Snifter?* Who is this woman?

Later, though her own nourishment seems to come only through the oxygen tube, she gets excited about dinner and insists that we all stay longer than usual at the table. Even my father submits to her authority. Though no one does anything special, she looks on with enjoyment, nodding approval, even when her head grows heavy and she rests it on a back of a propped forearm. There is the rug burn— unchanged. I remember her plunge through my hands and for an expanded moment feel all I've ever done is drop her. Then I catch a glimpse of her, seated in the same chair, years before, staring at a Christmas card with an expression of sad confusion. Later, I picked up the card, saw that it was from one of my paper route customers. "Michael is so expressive!" it read.

Now, Mom's downward gaze seems to be at something far beneath the tablecloth. For the first time I am staring not at my mother, but at someone I can't measure, someone who has read a different "card." I feel a sudden, desperate need to *bring her back.* I reach over, again place the Mets cap backwards upon her head.

"Ma, you look like Eminem," Natalie says.

She shrugs, stares back at me, and quickly appears to forget entirely about the cap. For a second, a bewilderment overtakes her face, and I see that I was wrong, that death leaves no card to ponder, but creeps up from behind, a sudden, chilling shoulder-tap.

She shakes her head, breaks out of her stupor, looks back at me warmly, but there is nothing to say. Natalie begins to cry. Dad gets up and leaves. I just sit there.

My father and I decide to take the dogs down to the beach, like we used to do.

"Well, she's stabilized, that's good," I say.

"She's telling her *brain*."

The remark sounds innocent, but it is a correction, an indirect reference to Pavlov. Over the years, Dad has instructed us all to "tell our brains" to resolve everything from depression to poison oak.

"How about we lay off all the theoretics, just for ten minutes?"

He shrugs. "It's all connected."

"But where does it leave her?"

He stares straight ahead, eyes wide to make sure that it is indeed a stop sign we are approaching. Since I've last seen him he's had cataract treatments. He reassures everyone that they have restored him to the keenness of youth, but this is hard to believe. "You sweep in with all this wisdom. But before she got sick how often did she hear from you?"

"And you have been there for her all of these years? *That's* what you call it?"

"There's so much you don't know," he admits. "You have no idea. All those years, seeing you grow up under her spell, knowing how *I* would have raised you."

"*Would* have? How great."

"We did our best."

"Oh—now there's a *we*."

It *is* a stop sign. My father has been stopped at it for half a minute. There is dead silence in the cab. We don't move.

"Leave her the fuck alone!" I scream. I see that I'm in the middle of the front seat, the seatbelt tight against my neck.

I have to get back to Berkeley—to school. I catch mom in a lucid moment to let her know of my plans. Her voice is low and raspy, her eyes recessed, a new vacancy to them. "Remember the bluejay that used to peck at the window every morning?"

23

"Maybe it was trying to tell me something," she says.

"That's a *raven*, Mom."

"Is your father taking you?"

"Natalie."

"Go to La Guardia. Kennedy's always a snarl." The conversation ends with a hug, but not much more than this distressing practicality.

At the airport, I tell Natalie that I'll make it back it a couple weeks.

"Will you?" she says. "Please."

Settled into my plane seat, it is these final conversations, all that *isn't* said, that gnaws at me. I manage to finish the Kundera, as a madcap Ben Stiller comedy runs soundlessly on the diminishing line of overhead screens. I will write her every day, I promise; gradually say all that needs to be said.

It is Natalie, then, who is left behind, all but alone, to give Mom the massages she can no longer feel, to read to her my scattered, aimless letters, to soothe her with lost memories. No more real connection, only Mom's anxious groans about the specific way she needs to be: propped up, let back, onto her stomach to ease the bedsores. With mammoth doses of morphine delivered by a home nurse, no more real pain except the vague humiliation of utter helplessness. And this is how Mom finally drifts off—only Natalie there, no final message, the world already too distant to fully depart from.

She is gone.

In my cramped Oakland apartment, I sit alone at my desk, self-conscious of every small motion, unsure what to do next. On the screen of my laptop is a scan of the second Poloroid, *the two of us in the shallow water, she, arm curled around my hip, smiling down at me as I stare off camera,* next to it, one sent from Natalie's phone: *frayed Mets cap backwards on her head, chin resting on the back of her arm, oxygen tube fixed to her nose, eyes fixed on the camera,* eyes so sunken and deep that they follow me as I get up and move about the room, walls pressing in on me. I have refused to return for the memorial; I am done dealing with my father.

A remote is on the floor. I pick it up, scan for something to distract me, but there are too many channels, too many smiling faces. I settle on a 90's hoop game on ESPN Classic—Knicks and Bulls—that brings me back to a time when rosters and statistics were riveting drama. But the long-ago game is coming to a close, too, the seconds dwindling, until the station segues to an interview with Jimmy Breslin, longtime beat reporter for the Daily News, speaking about some colleague.

I flip through more stations, more faces, but I can't stand them. I wind up back where I was—on ESPN Classic. There is at least something about Breslin's face, a haggardness that makes him bearable, like white noise. And something else that is unusual—he seems to be upset. Even the youthful anchor has taken notice.

"…there was the whole early crew…," Breslin rambles, "then, I guess we drew apart. That whole friendship with Bobby Fischer, I didn't get."

The anchor turns to the camera uncomfortably, and says, "Once again, ladies and gentlemen, Dick Schaap, American sportswriter and author, dead at sixty seven, following complications from hip-replacement surgery." Then he turns back to Breslin, tries to cue him. "You miss him, Jimmy."

The sparse words appear to fatigue Breslin, who merely stares at the floor, and quickly his face is replaced by a photo montage of Schaap amidst various interviews, all to plaintive music.

I stand there in the middle of my cramped room, hands pressed into my pockets, staring at the frame of photos, but I want Breslin back, if only for another moment. That haggard, broken face of Breslin.

Der Leiermann

Across the street, the bearded man slouches
on his backpack beneath an ice covered awning.
Surplus coat, surplus cycles of freeze and thaw,

moth-eaten cap. His chapped hands search
for the chords to some Lennon song, guitar slung
across his body, strap frayed, missing a string.

The crosswalk signal flashes red, green, red,
against his frets. People rush from the city bus,
past the man, refuse his bloodshot eyes, focus
on the salted sidewalk ahead.

I cross, toss a bill into his empty case.
Forget the recipe for Coq au Vin.
Forget which wine to serve for dinner at six.

Period

She said she wasn't in the mood for anything, not even oral, not on a day when her flow was thick as the candle wax from that unscented chunk in the bathroom, as full as her tumbler of cheap wine. He said, "Fine, you go ahead and flow. Go ahead an get drunk, too. It's like you're drunk just on being a woman." She flicked her cigarette butt at him and told him to fuck himself. He called her a mean drunk. He said, "You sit there and you flood, sit there while you garden your fingers."

She said, "What the hell are you talking about?"

And he said, "You clip and you hedge. It's like some sort of zen with you." She studied her nails, set aside her emery board. He said, "I don't even care."

He changed his mind. Instead of abrasive page-turning, the leaves in his book chafing against each other, or leaving her her zen to walk away and disappear, instead of these, he slapped his book shut and he leaned forward and grinned. He said, "No—You know what? It turns me on."

She said, "Stop it."

He said, "No, it's like you have little vampire lips, all slippery and evil-looking, and it excites me." He scooted to the edge of his chair, leered at her. "They smell like mud in some fertile swamp, like moth larvae. What's the word? Pupating." She shifted, crossed her legs. He lowered his voice, looked around the empty living room. He said, "You know what I want? I want to drive your blood to a lather. Go ahead, show me what's so fucking nasty."

He sat back against his chair and threw an ankle across his knee, readjusted his book. He wasn't smiling anymore. He shook his head once and read. But she wasn't ignoring him. She eyed him like she eyed her patients at the psychical therapy clinic; she uncrossed her legs, let her knees fall open slightly, and leaned toward him. The rings of green encasing her irises looked black, not just the pupils empty but the whole of both eyes, those normally emerald nimbi now obsidian, now glistening.

She said nothing.

She stood from her chair and stepped over to face him, put her thumbs in the collected waistbands of her green sweat pants and her gray biker shorts and her thick cotton panties and she tugged down on them, dropped it all to her feet, dark pad and old panties and everything. She looked at him; he did not look at her. He couldn't. He laid his book in his lap and watched her feet, the pile of clothes, the dark stain like a bullseye in there.

After a minute, a minute and a half, she bent and hauled up all those clothes back around her waist, worked the elastic back and forth over her hips in a way that, in reverse, would have had him panting, and she left him. Staring at the floor.

Refusal

The same point, critically hit
as always. Should or shouldn't
is the real question.
The coin flips.
Heads. For the 253rd time in a row
I put the phone down, unused.
Maybe one day
I will understand why it is always wet
after it rains.

Cold Water on Blood

This morning, one of my Greenville relatives called to say that my cousin and childhood playmate, Anne Dittwilder, suddenly died yesterday in Phoenix. To occupy my hands while digesting the news, I weeded the roses bordering my fishpond. But my care was not with my roses, and, before I knew it, a thorn seized my forearm. It made a deep scratch. Watching the blood disappear over the curve of my arm, I recognized that the cut was inevitable and more than coincidence. As I cleaned it under a stream of cold water, my tears spilled over Anne's death, and also over the death, years ago, of my husband, Paul.

Once we reached adulthood, the only time I saw Anne was at Paul's funeral. We were only 37 when he died. The shock turned me to stone. At the service and reception, I couldn't feel my own body, and I wasn't even yet aware that Paul had killed himself. We'd borrowed money to start a video rental business and then had a streak of bad luck -- a busted water pipe, inadequate insurance, an employee who was stealing. One Sunday evening in the middle of April, Paul's car hit a tree. Initially, it looked like an accident, more bad luck. But when my father examined the lack of curve in the road, the absence of skid marks, and, finally, weeks later, Paul's books, there wasn't much doubt in his mind. By that time, I'd begun grieving. But I never saw Anne again, and Christmas cards are no place to thank anyone for the odd kind of help she gave me that started my journey toward healing.

When we were children, Anne lived in Greenville, Kentucky, and I lived in Nashville, Tennessee. Our fathers were first cousins with a close bond, so every summer Anne and I spent a week in each other's homes. Her family lived on a tree-lined street in a white house with a screened-in porch across the front. She had two sisters, one very young, and the other, Laura, old enough, on the night I'm recalling, to be out on a date. So Anne, one of her friends and I were sitting on a metal swing on the porch, talking in the twilight. I can't remember, except for curly hair, what the friend looked like, but Anne was blonde and freckled, and her features (and, probably, mine) were still a little flat with childhood. We all were wearing shorts and white cotton shirts, and, somehow, during our conversation, I cut my thumb on the swing. The blood flowed quickly and brightly, and so frightened me that I flung it into the air, and onto my shirt and the shirt of Anne's friend. I was as alarmed by staining the girl's clothing as I was by bleeding. I was sure her mother would be angry with me. I apologized over and over, while my thumb continued to leak. It was Anne who got up, went into the house and, evidently without alerting an adult, came out with two rags and a bowl of cold water. The smaller rag she dipped into the water and wrapped around my thumb. The larger she dipped into the water and used to wipe the blood off our clothes, the swing and the planks of the porch. She kept saying, "Always use cold water on blood. Warm water sets the stain." I was sort of a tomboy and had cut myself before, and the fact that Anne had that information, when I didn't, seemed mysterious to me; like she had crossed over to a world I didn't even know existed. I felt even younger than ten, and remember feeling like Anne, older by a year, had a greater edge on me than she usually did.

After the blood was wiped away, the friend went home, and Anne and I went for a walk, me with my thumb still wrapped in the rag and my ego bruised by the mess I'd made. We headed toward the church on the corner solely because Anne's grandmother lived in the opposite direction. This isn't to say anything derogatory about her, or about the sister who lived with her. Both were my great aunts, and I was as fond of them as a child could be, considering the age difference, the perfume and the obligation to kiss. And Anne and I weren't yet up to anything. We avoided supervision out of principle. So we walked in the direction of the church, circumvented a large oak that grew in the sidewalk and turned the corner. When we did, we saw that the church's front door was cracked open. Naturally, we went in.

31

It was cooler inside than out, and the sanctuary was dim and smelled like clothes in a winter closet. Anne said, "Let's go up to the altar."

"What if we're caught?"

"We'll pretend we're lost."

I must've looked doubtful. She said, "Don't be a chicken."

That was convincing, of course. I was always trying to prove my mettle with Anne. So I marched right up the aisle, climbed a few steps and stopped beside the pulpit. I turned toward the pews and belted, "Well, since my baby left me, I found a new place to dwell. It's down at the end of Lonely Street at Heartbreak Hotel." I swung my hips, too. I'd seen Elvis on TV, and although they wouldn't show him from the waist down, we'd all heard what was going on below the camera. Looking back, I know I picked one of Elvis' songs because my parents had a television, but Anne's didn't.

However, my triumph was short-lived. My voice reverberated off the walls of that hollow sanctuary and hit my ears like an accusation of sin. Anne was so stunned that she said, "Well, smack my behind!" That reverberated, too. And after those waves died, we heard steps coming in our direction. We froze like little possums. The steps grew louder, and near enough to distinguish two sets. I was closer to the pulpit than Anne was. I could see it was hollow and that the space inside was large enough to hide us. I motioned wildly to Anne and ducked into the hole. She stuffed in next to me tightly; her elbow jabbed my stomach, her shoulder bone poked my chest where my left breast would've been if I'd had one. I held my rag-wrapped thumb up to protect it.

The footsteps padded into the sanctuary and shuffled around. One set walked away from us and came back. A man's voice said, "The front door was open. They're gone."

"Who do you think it was?" a woman responded.

"Probably children. It sounded squeaky."

"Should we check around?"

"No, we're safe. Come here. I've waited six days."

After that, we heard more shuffling, whispering, and some thumping that seemed particularly strange. I tried to imagine an explanation, couldn't, and, to keep myself still, focused on Anne's smell. I decided she smelled like a sack of potatoes. I thought about potatoes until the thumping stopped, and sighing and murmuring started. Then my leg cramped. I changed its position. Anne readjusted and bumped against the pulpit.

The man said, "It's nothing. Don't worry."

"Are you sure?"

"Positive. This place creaks on its own. That was terrific. You're saving my life."

I didn't see how thumping around in a church could save anyone's life. I'd heard sermons on being saved, but my parents tried to keep me quiet in church, and that thumping didn't seem like what my minister was talking about. After that, there was more murmuring and some rustling. Finally, the man said, "Thursday, same time?"

"Okay. Harold's gone 'til Friday."

"How about here?"

"Don't you feel it sort of sinful here?"

"Most people would say it's sinful anywhere we do it. But, Marlene, I swear, you're saving my life. I need you like food and air."

After that, their voices lowered, they shuffled some more, walked close to the pulpit and out the door they'd entered. Until their steps faded, neither Anne nor I moved, but when we tumbled out of our hole, I whispered, "What do you think they were doing?"

Anne literally put her fist in her mouth. Still, I could tell she was laughing at me. I said, "What's so funny?" She doubled over. I said, "Tell me. That's not nice." I shook her shoulder.

She rose up. "Don't you know?"

"Sure. I just wanta be sure you know." That was a lie, of course. But I did know that not knowing was as bad as bleeding on people's clothes.

So we both agreed we knew what they were doing, and we crept around trying to discover where they'd done it. We didn't find any clues. But we decided to locate a hiding place with a better view and to return on Thursday. In her own church, Anne sat with other children up in the balcony, and the church we were in had a balcony, too. So we went up there to find a place to hide. That railing was wood, and between the panels were slits an inch wide. Those slits provided an unobstructed view below to the pews.

On Thursday, we were about three feet apart peering through slits when they came in, him first. He locked the side door they'd entered, checked the one in the opposite wall and then walked down a side aisle, disappearing beneath us, checking, I figured, the front door. While he made those rounds, she went to the fourth row of pews. I wasn't happy she chose the fourth row. It gave us a good view, but I sat with my parents in the fourth row at our church and it seemed to me like they were taking our seats. I still didn't know what they were planning to do, but I did know it was sneaky and naughty and, since our last visit, Anne and I had had several conversations that had run, in short: "I can't believe anybody would do that in a church" and, "Me either. They could get in a lot of trouble."

Well, they went to it quickly. She settled on the cushions; he pushed her skirt up, unbuckled his belt and pushed his trousers down. He got on top of her and grunted, his bare bottom exposed. Then he caved in on her and went still. They stayed like that mumbling, until he grasped the back of the pew in front and rose up. We could see his boy's part as clearly as if it'd been a communion cup. I was marveling at it when he said, "You're bleeding! Why didn't you tell me?" He held his cup in his hand and inspected it.

She pushed her skirt down. "I wasn't bleeding before. You must've shaken it loose."

"Don't blame me. There's blood everywhere."

"I can't help it. I always start heavy."

"It's your mess. Figure out what to do."

"We'll use my slip." She fumbled, shimmied and drew the slip off over her feet. He grabbed it and wiped himself. I was so transfixed by him cleaning his penis that I didn't notice what she was doing. But I heard her begin crying. He said, "Stop that. You've got us in enough trouble. Let's get out of here." He handed her the slip, tucked himself in and zipped up. He turned toward the door.

She stood up, straightened her clothes and swiped the cushion with her slip. "Wait for me," she said, and quickly followed him. She shut the door behind them.

While I was still trying to figure out what had happened, Anne said, "That's Mrs. Edwards. Lordy."

"Who's he?"

"Oh, he's the preacher."

"The preacher?" I couldn't have been more dismayed. Not only was he doing something clearly abnormal, he was doing it in a church, with a woman who probably wasn't his wife. On top of that, my father was the chair of the committee that hired our ministers and I knew that kind of behavior wasn't what he was looking for when he interviewed people. I said, "Should we tell somebody?"

"Like who?"

"The hiring committee?"

Anne looked at me like I'd suggested we notify Martians. I said, "Well, who do you think we should tell?"

"Nobody. We'll make trouble for ourselves and everybody else. We need to fix the cushion." With that Anne was up and headed toward the stairs. I followed her, more out of bewilderment than sense of shared purpose.

When we got to the ground floor, Anne was as busy as a moth circling a light bulb. She checked the stain and tried to turn the cushion. It was attached to the bench. She went to the altar, pulled wilted flowers out of a vase and squeezed their stems so that water dripped back into the container. She laid the flowers on the floor. She held up the altar cloth, inspected it, and said, "You carry the vase." By that time, she was on her way to the fourth row of pews.

Anne scrubbed and scrubbed. I just held the vase. Eventually, she stood up, backed off, and inspected the cushion from a distance. She whispered, "I wish we could turn the light on."

I shook my head.

"I know. I was just wishing. Let's put this stuff back and get out of here."

She laid the cloth back on the altar, but set the flowers and vase on their sides, so that, in our minds at least, the stain on the altar cloth looked like it had come from the vase being turned over. Then we quietly hurried to the front door. It was locked. There wasn't a key. Anne pushed and pulled the door anyway. I listened to my heart thump. Finally she said, "We're trapped."

I suggested we try the windows. Four were large and stained glass, but there were smaller ones, too, and one of them was open. It wasn't large, but neither were we. And beneath it outside grew a thick bush. We jumped on top of the bush. Anne grabbed my arm and said, "Come on."

We ran until we got in sight of her house. There on the front swing sat her parents. We slowed to a walk and I concentrated solely on catching my breath, as Anne dealt with her parents for us and I dealt with mine. We greeted hers like we were glad to see them and Anne told them a story about how we'd been at the baseball diamond, watching boys play ball. She named several children I didn't know. After that, we were told to take our baths and to go to bed. It wasn't until Anne tiptoed over to my twin and got in with me that I said, "Do you think he hurt her bad?"

"I don't think so."

"What about the blood?"

"That happens every month."

I didn't believe that. "Then why did he act so surprised?"

"You're not supposed to have sex when it happens."

I said, "Oh, yeah, I forgot." Then, for fear of asking a question that would give me away, I suggested we go to sleep.

The next day, we chewed on whether we should tell Anne's big sister, Laura. We decided against it; Laura had turned fifteen and was acting like she was better than we were. We didn't even discuss telling Anne's parents. And at the weekend, mine came and took us to

Nashville. There we spent our days playing croquette and canasta, and our nights watching *I Love Lucy* and *Ed Sullivan*. Caught up in new activities, we didn't talk about the preacher and his friend.

In the next few years, of course, my body changed. And for a long time, whenever I used cold water on my own monthly blood, the memory mostly served to embarrass me about how naïve I'd been. After that, there was a time in graduate school when I employed the memory to rouse my righteous indignation over the hypocrisy of the institutional church and the sexism of men. But I grew out of that; and I didn't think much about any of it at all for a long time, until Paul killed himself.

His face had gone through the windshield; his chest had been crushed by the steering wheel. A few days after his funeral, the M.E. gave me a sack that held his wallet, his jewelry and his clothes. His collar and the front of his shirt were red with blood. I locked myself in our bathroom, and despite my mother and my closest friend pleading through the door, I stayed in there alone. I scrubbed and scrubbed Paul's shirt under a stream of cold water until I washed all of his blood out and down the drain. Then I started grieving.

Match

She pairs cowboy boots with short skirts, wears the tightest tank tops. Wants everything to be out in the open. *Honest*, she'll say, and look at you with her sky blue, cornflower blue, blue like the top half of ocean water somewhere tropical blue eyes. They will pull you in like an undertow, knock you over, knock you flat on your back until you're staring up at her, her strong thighs planted on either side of your face so that she can lower herself onto your mouth like an open sunflower.

You're left as breathless as the playground merry-go-round. Fix your eyes on a point in the distance, hold tight as she goes spinning by, floating past all those outstretched fingertips like a field of dandelion heads gone to seed.

After she breaks the dishes, she sings lullabies, weaves melodies like blankets, like nets, like cocoons. Like being embraced by a hammock in the heat after noon with fresh-squeezed lemonade damp on your lips.

She won't cry yet, standing there again on your doorstep. *A matching pair*, she says, a bruise circling each eye.

You've seen this before. You've arranged the getaway car, bought the bus ticket, paid for cab fare, brought the horse and tied it up to the old oak, tipped your hat and held out your hand like you're asking her to dance.

You should see the other guy, she says. Takes the ice wrapped in a flannel shirt. Lays her head in your lap, blue eyes looking up, as you touch the dried salt from her black-eyed-Susan face.

Meet Me at the Monkey Bars

Dear Laura,

I'm sorry I didn't kiss you back. The timing was severely awkward, and to be quite honest, I've never been much of a fan of public displays of affection. With everyone standing around watching, I would have been far too self-conscious, and I'm not sure you would have been pleased with the end result.

Plus, I was only 5 years old.

That's really gotta count for something, in my defense. Sure, you were the same age, but I was small for my age, and you towered over me. And, anyhow, girls mature faster than boys.

I hope that now you don't hold it against me. I guess we're, what, 27 years later, so it's doubtful you still hold a grudge. Just know that it wasn't because you weren't pretty, because you were. You had the prettiest long hair in school, and I mean that. Other girls, well, they just had long hair that trailed off down below their asses, just hanging there limp like a novelty, but you, you Laura, you did something with it. It sparkled, although I'm sure our arts and crafts time probably helped fill it with glitter, but to me, it was pure stardust. I'm not sure what you did to it — maybe just brushed it — but it worked.

I also liked that you smelled like glue.

Anyway, Laura, I hope you're doing well and have found someone who will kiss you underneath the monkey bars. Me? Well, I'm still looking. Maybe I'll try the swing set …

Sincerely,

P.S. I should probably clarify that I didn't mean a literal swing set. I don't regularly pick up women (or kids, for that matter) at the neighborhood playgrounds. So please don't think awful of me.

P.S.S. Reading back, I see again where I should note that I was kidding about picking up kids at a playground. I shouldn't joke about that. As far as I know, you could've had a child molested or kidnapped from a playground, and my attempts at humor are only bringing back those terrible memories. Which, I guess, I'm also doing here by keeping on talking about it. Except allow me to say, if you did have a kid stolen (I know that you don't "steal" a child, but it would have been odd to have had "kid" and "kidnapped" right next to each other, although I guess I could have gone with "child" and "kidnapped" instead), I hope you and your family have healed from the loss and have had more kids to replace him. Or her, I guess, if it was a girl.

And if you didn't suffer a kidnapping, congratulations!

Best wishes.

Over Exposure

Ansel says it's ok to be exposed in the darkroom
red light's actually blinding and everyone here is lined up naked
anyway

He speaks as if he holds a secret just under his Adam's apple
Ignoring that we came to bring something like it from
blankness

Ignoring that mine may be prettier, his more red and yours wet
and ready to go
He knows that we're all standing around here trying to get bigger

growing vulnerable in our raw condition, propagating in dark
exposure
and getting off because when we walk out there and hit those
walls

Everyone will know what we did in the dark, what he held below
his throat
will be glad I came, exposed, hung- there- we'll die having spread
wide our names

Rejoice

"THIS IS VANITY. THIS IS A COUNTRY OF DOGS. THIS IS THE REASON SAINTS DIE AND ABORT TO THE AFTERLIFE," Quori wrote a rough draft of a new poem in his Moleskine journal as the church organ played, echoing hymns of mourning throughout the gothic building for the late Andrew Dell. He stood in the back with Benny, the seats being taken up early by closer family and friends than them. As for those two, they had grown up in Manhattan around Andrew Dell, gone to school with him, and had parents that were good friends with his parents, though they couldn't attend that day. Having gone to Turks and Caicos for the holidays on a joint trip, their parents could not have planned a more unfortunate time to take a vacation.

Andrew Dell got killed by driving drunk in Manhattan, a place already too well known for its exceedingly dangerous and aggravated motorists. The driver in the other lane didn't even see him coming. Even more unfortunately for the families and friends involved, his death occurred the week before Christmas day, while celebrating the homecoming of some of his closest friends from their respective colleges.

Now the red advent candles glowed in their green wreath, suspended from a thick silver chain, as the priest in a bold purple robe, blessed the crowd and Andrew's body by shaking and swaying a golden container of incense through the aisles. Two Christmas trees were on either side of the altar, Blue Firs, with gold and red ribbons wrapped around their prickly branches. Each contained silver stars on their very tops. The burning wicks overlapping the soothing aroma of the incense and the trees wafted through the two friend's nostrils as they stood in the back, letting the humming of the massive pipe organ regurgitate itself through their cloudy heads. Had they known Andrew Dell a bit better, there would have been more mourning on their part. However, they held a different perspective, drawn back from the closed in walls of a compact social life, which drifts one away from the more grounding emotions and into a state of despair upon the witness of death.

"Hey, Benny," Quori whispered at his friend, as Mr. Dell took to the podium up on the altar. The casket lay in front of the man, open, exposing the eerie attempt at reconstructing the corpse into a handsome son, and beautiful relic of a past life, with a suit and makeup, hands folded. Men and Women sobbed in the audience, as Mr. Dell introduced himself needlessly and began praising his son's existence.

"What's up man?" Benny whispered back, taking his gaze off the altar to glance at his friend for a moment. A man in all black, sitting in front of where they stood, turned around in his seat to glare at the two in disapproval of their whispers. Seeing they didn't care, and not wanting to make a scene, he reabsorbed himself into the speech.

"Do you remember what Andy was like in high school?" Quori asked.

"Yeah, I think so. High school is kind of a blur these days, man," he huffed air through his nose, attempting the laughing equivalent of a whisper to show his good intentions.

"No man," Quori said, disregarding Ben's laugh, "Like... Do you *really* remember what Andy was like in high school?" Images of football players in blue and red uniforms, clashing into each other with helmets at the start of the play ran through Ben's mind. Andrew was a quarterback and tossed the ball with ease and precision, as the drum line pounded beats through the small depression in the park where the field was built; creating a tribal soundtrack to the athleticism of the schoolyard's finest. He thought of the girls Andrew Dell crooned with his large truck, and extensive hip hop and hard rock collection he blasted on his way to school on a regular basis. He thought of the rumors of his Friday nights, the ones that Ben and Quori were not allowed to be a part of. Sexual activity before everyone else. Sexual prowess. Wholly endowed with everything a young man needed to prove himself to what one perceived to be the trials of being an adult.

"He was a player man," Benny replied, "A beast."

"Yeah, but that's not what *I* remember," said Quori. "*I* remember a guy who turned off the lights in the bathroom on the kid with Down syndrome, screaming and scaring him out into the halls with his Special Ed dick out, pants around his ankles, making everyone laugh. I remember the guy who punched me in the face during a Rec. Center basketball game because I blocked his shot at the final moment. And I couldn't say anything because our parents were friends." Ben stood staring out at the casket, recollecting, as Mr. Dell continued his speech at the podium.

"Yeah, but you have to let that shit go, Quori. He's dead."

"No use in glorifying him though. Like his jaded father is doing right up there."

"*And I can still remember that time on his tenth birthday, when Andrew refused to use the money I gave him for the candy shop, so he could pass it off to a homeless man. I ask you, would you have done the same?*" Mr. Dell questioned, reciting his son's minor life achievements, weaved delicately through heartfelt stories and memories.

"People just like to remember the good things man. It's uplifting," reasoned Benny.

"We'll why can't we also remember the bad?" asked Quori. The man sitting in front of the two had then had enough of their whispers, though he couldn't make out what it was they were saying. He adjusted his seat in the pew to turn around as the wood creaked awkwardly under Mr. Dell's solemn words. He thoroughly hushed Ben and Quori up, with a finger to his lips. The song on the organ changed, and a harsh sob of Andrew Dell's mother sounded out as the tone in Mr. Dell's voice rose in accompaniment to the mellow music.

He grasped both hands on the grips of the colossal red wooden doors. The gothic church was sandwiched within five feet of two separate gray high rise buildings. Its steeples no longer towered in the sky like they did years ago. As he pushed the doors open, walking into the cloud of warmth and scent of the advent candles, the wind swept in with him, in a gust that brought in a light bed of snow. The crowd all turned their heads to see who had arrived so late, before looking back to Mr. Dell and his speech. He still stood at the podium, stretching out his talk as long as he could. The audience still mourned and cried. Ben and Quori stood watching the newcomer as Andrew's father shared anecdotes of his son's life. The young man in the back dipped his calloused hands into the pool of holy water by the entrance, making the sign of the cross before walking casually past the two friends and down the aisle. His face had looked so familiar to the two, though they didn't know where they could have ever seen him before. It was textured with large pores and various blackheads and marks. His eyes were heavy, brown and cold, with bushy wrinkled brows. His face held determination in it and his expression seemed vaguely reminiscent of someone they once knew. "Did we go to high school with that guy?" asked Benny looking at his friend.

"What? Oh, I dunno," replied Quori. He was too busy pulling out his Moleskine from his tight back pocket.

"THIS IS HOLINESS. THIS IS SPARING THE CHILD. THIS IS EVERY REASON THE CONTRADICTIONS OF MAN GO UNNOTICED," Quori jotted down as Mr. Dell spoke.

"And most of all, Andrew was one of the biggest people persons I ever met. There was not a single guy I knew, or girl, who didn't admire, love, or look up to him in some way." Mrs. Dell smiled knowingly.

That's when the gun shot rang out.

It resonated in the hollow church as the organ paused, leaving that lasting melancholy echo of vibrating notes and chords in the rafters. Andrew's father dropped to the floor of the altar, and the people of the church screamed out in shock and fear to add to their sadness.

"Come on!" Quori said through his teeth in a craze, grabbing Benny's arm through his white collared shirt, "Let's get the fuck out of here!" More shots rang out. People cried out in pain, dropped to the floor or ran for their lives. No one moved to help Mr. Dell. The mother was nowhere to be found and the Priest hid with his back to the podium breathing heavily as Ben and Quori slipped out the front door. Outside, the snow was heavy like a white frozen blanket to cool down their racing hearts. Most of the people outside didn't even have the time to grab their coats or jackets. People screamed and ran through the street, stopping traffic as brakes screeched and cars slid through the ice and snow of the Upper East Side's roads. Sirens sounded.

There was no one left inside the church, and the lone gunman kneeled before the crucified statue of Christ and mumbled warm prayers with his hands clasped together on the handle of the gun. As the police busted open the doors with excessive force, and dashed down the aisles past the empty pews and scattered bodies, the gunman pulled the trigger. Blood, brains and tissue sprayed out the back of his head onto the pews, and his body fell forward, sprawled out before the idolized judgment of Christ, who looked down at him with sullen eyes.

"WHAT THE *FUCK* WAS THAT!?" Benny yelled in a stupor, feeling safer now that the wall of squad cars separated them and the old sandwiched Church. The snow dotted out the sky. Everything was white. Everything looked pure. But inside the gothic church were bloodstains and tears, clothes draped on wooden pews, and candles burning on top of the aroma of the dead.

"No fucking clue, man," replied Quori, panting with his hands on his knees. Benny held his arms crossed, shivering. It looked like he was crying.

"Well Merry fucking Christmas Quori!" he yelled, "Jesus Christ! FUCK."

They walked down the street in shock, not even really knowing where they were or where they were going. They just had to get away.

"I wonder what they'll say about the gunman at his funeral. He must have had a fucked up life," said Quori, staring harshly into Benny's eyes. "After all, it's best to remember the uplifting things." They were both extremely stressed, passing bodegas and grocery stores, apartment buildings and a coffee shop. The sound of an ambulance rang off down the street as cars rushed by, and the white snow fell from the white sky. There was a lack of the sun, but somehow the earth still held light.

"Fuck you, man," replied Benny, "Let's go in here for a second." The two entered the coffee shop, wiping their shoes on the mat in the doorway. They faced death. They faced eternity. They faced the rest of their lives, and countless funerals to come. Quori stared out the window as Benny sipped his coffee, coming to terms that maybe there was some power in remembering the good.

"LET US REJOICE," he wrote quickly in his journal, trying to convince himself under his other words in chicken scratch handwriting. But still, as the snow fell, the people passed and the warmth of the coffee shop set into his frigid skin, he wasn't sure if he actually believed it. He wasn't sure of anything at all.

If Water Were Religion

What if water were religion:

not its abundance, as if it

were a magnificent finiteness,

ream to bolt, fold to bias;

or if we celebrated scarcity,

for it once bubbled and teased

as though its source essence

was an insatiable mathematical

formula due to an early trauma

that tumbled through the mulch.

Regardless there would be the

weight and depth of it, and

acolytes would slave away with

chips and chisels, to reach the core

of its inverse philosophy, its currency

that is shell and center, an enigma

within a dichotomy that is both

a god and his descendant:

Then we would not honor it with

petals or ashes, but with the silver

redacted from negatives, and when

the laundry's clean and the bones

have been swept in by the sons,

we would use water for stashing

evidence, the disputations and contradictions.

Florida

Grandma said lying runs in the family, but Dad didn't call them lies.

"We'll fly to Florida," he'd say when sleet pinged the windows at night. "There's always bright oranges and grapefruit hanging on the trees like little suns."

"Even now?" I'd ask, tucked under blankets not yet warm.

"We'll pick them and walk along the beach. Let the juice drip down our chins."

"I wasn't blind to the truth," Grandma would say later as she looked out the window at the shiny black streets and the dark wet night. Then she'd stay up late telling me stories about my grandfather through purple wrinkled lips.

Perhaps I should've listened, but in my head I walked through crashing waves and caught ropes of fish-smelling seaweed and let the cuffs of my pants get wet in the salty ocean.

My grandmother always talked about my grandfather on dark winter nights after Dad had gone to sleep or else he'd yell, "Ma, quit telling her that junk." And then, "Ruby, go to bed," as if shouting that through thin walls made him the type of dad who wouldn't walk away.

"It was Susan," he'd say many years later over the phone when it was just Grandma and me and had been for a long time. "It was when Susan brought Hillary into my office." As if Susan was the one to blame.

I watched while he packed the one black suitcase. There weren't suits or ties like one of his business trips but t-shirts and shorts and a pair of sandals I'd never seen. I thought of his white legs and the black hairs that sprouted and curled over them. I couldn't imagine him without his black socks on.

"But you promised you'd take me," I said. "Not her."

He sighed the way he always did whenever Grandma or me said anything about her. Then he hefted the suitcase off the bed and walked down the hall.

"Just like his father," Grandma said to the night window. "Everyone said so the day he was born, but I wouldn't believe it."

"Ma quit talking like that. It'll only be for a few days." Then to me he said, "You have your grandmother."

I looked at her still looking out the dark window, seeing things I couldn't see.

I turned to him. "Hillary?" I said. "What kind of a name is Hillary?"

"I'll be back soon," he said and closed the door behind him. But of course he wasn't.

Two weeks later I got a postcard in the mail with "Florida" written in yellow cursive letters over a background painted blue. Inside the letters were drawings of palm trees, cresting waves, and trees with yellow and golden balls of fruit.

"They always take them to Florida," Grandma said and went back to her seat by the window.

My Bird of Paradise

a visit to my grandfather in Mexico

I saw him last week

on the patio, his tan off-set

by palm leaves and banana

skins. I didn't notice

his wrinkles – as if the sun

had pulled him away

from his eighty-seven years.

But his shoulders were still

beak-curved and pained.

Lazy off the tiles and nestled

in the musted bark of a tree he grew

a blossom from its leaf hatches,

his living stained glass of green

and guava orange.

Within the origami purple plume

was a single stain of dew.

This is for you, he said, my little dying
paradise now perched in the vase
with common yellow peonies, a pair
of scissors on the table.

I couldn't tell him to let it breathe
where it had been. There was a margarita
in my hand, too much salt, lime
pulp sticking in my throat.

With sap on our fingers we learned
it wasn't dew at all.

The Immutable

I moved to the window in order to gather a greater perception of what was happening. A vacant rumbling was transforming my world. I could not count the number of explosions that bombarded the earth. I knew that these violent disruptions were subject to the system that they slowly dismantled; each gust of power was defined by its failure to abolish some cognizable degree of truth. I was very confused. The room had rearranged itself thoroughly, into nonsense. Objects that were normally so conventional that I should dismiss them had mutated into flickering vestiges of their former significance. They had begun to mean nothing that I could perceive categorically. Yet, that was not what they were precisely. They were, in some way that I could not explain, different from how I had once known them.

My house was set close to a proud cliff that jutted out from a dark mountain. I had known a languid stream to spill over the cliff into the rivulet below. The cliff seemed relatively desiccated, and the water lapped patiently against the base of the mountain. The day rose over the cliff, and a ray of sun passed through the window. It fell onto my chest then cast my image back through the glass. The image mimicked every one of my movements. I lowered my head, and it bowed to me. As I raised my arm, and stretched my hand, it waved, sheepishly. I marveled at this likeness, and together we played. An explosion erupted near the image, causing a void where, previously, the ground was solid, and nearly level. It severed the ears from my image, and destroyed its tongue. The window was partially shattered. I heard what I thought was the sound of my voice. My image began speaking with its fingers. I could not interpret what was said. There was another awful crash, and its fingers were amputated. The monster looked at its hands; then it stumbled into a deep hole, and disappeared. I mulled over these bizarre circumstances, weighing them, one against the other, in order to gather some idea of what was happening. I could only perceive the suffering of chaos. I realized that I had been screaming.

Every house was a near replication of my own. My neighbors were shouting from their windows, when the bombardment finally ended. Their jumbled antiphony gasped and shrieked like a choir of startled pheasants. I called out to the others: *What is...* Their voices collided with one another. Could they not understand me? The explosions ceased, and for a brief moment, every voice was silenced. I could hear an unruly noise slapping at the foot of the dark mountain. The waterfall! We all stepped outside of our houses, and began speaking in different directions. There were, it seemed, many conversations stirring among us. One man, five houses down from my own, pointed past me toward the mountain, and spoke of killing. A man three houses down heard the first man, by way of the neighbor between them. He pointed to the stream and spoke- to his left and to his right- of drowning. At hearing this, the man in the house next to mine ran past my door, and splashed into the water. I went to fetch him from the stream, but he refused my hand. He struck my face with great force. I did not know what to make of this. I could hear the clamor of men quarrelling in every direction. I looked up, into the molten sun, and decided to leave them.

I followed the winding rivulet through the countryside, noting the numerous markers I encountered along the way. Each post was emblazoned with a unique and indecipherable symbol. After some time, the number of symbols on each marker increased, so that there was one and another. I recognized each character when I saw it again. I considered the next post. It was marked by a symbol that I had passed once already, and once more before that; it was marked, just as well, with a different symbol. This character had appeared only once before, when the number of symbols on each marker increased. I considered the next post. One of its symbols had appeared on the previous marker, and once before that, and another time before that; there was also a different symbol, like there was on the previous marker. This symbol had appeared more often than the others, far too often for me to reflect on each instance at once.

Beyond the marker, the rivulet fed into a much larger river. The water churned, and folded in on itself where the streams intersected. The rapids appeared to increase in violence further downstream. I noticed a dirt road, off in the distance. I walked along the road for a long time. Only by the increasing darkness, could I quantify the overwhelming expanse that I traveled. I was not far from collapsing, when I reached another town. I had never experienced such exhaustion. The people were kind. A very nice man lived in the first house. He fed me, and sent me to rest at a neighbor's. The next day I left the town. I began to reach one town after the other. Each was situated in close proximity to the next. Upon leaving each town, I noticed that my speech had changed. I could not say how this occurred, nor could I explain why; but I knew all that were necessary, in each instance that it was required. The words were dragged through my mouth, as though I were vomiting a series of swollen appendages. They scraped away the surface of my tongue, and created many uncomfortable blisters. When I could bear the pain no longer, I refused to talk, unless it was necessary. The people in the towns began to mistrust me, because I said very little. They shunned me, and they stole my motivation to speak. I was frightened by the thought of becoming lost again, but I preferred that anxiety to the torment of another disdainful population.

I stole away from the road that connected all of the towns. I walked into the wilderness, stamping out an unprecedented trail, until I reached a great field. There was a large sign at the edge of the field. It read, distinctly: *There is no language beyond this point.* The inscription seemed to imply that I was in the midst of language. I attempted to sink my hand into the field, but my fingers refused to slip between the tall blades of grass. I ran my palm against them. What did they mean? I considered the field itself. It twisted and swayed in every direction that the wind suggested, but it would not bend freely to the bulk of my mass. I understood that these countless thousands of small parts contributed to the unified whole that was the field. I realized then that each blade was an inseparable part of the total field. Once I knew this I could not unknow it. The field could be nothing other than what it was, regardless of how it came to be. I could not know, nor will it to be a duck, a postcard, a bicycle, or a dinner plate. These fantasies were dismissed as quickly as they were conceived. They were digested into the memory.

I thought I should walk around the field. At the first step, my foot collided with an immovable object. I saw my father lying before me. His head was turned on its side, and his jaw was hung open, listlessly. A stump of pink flesh dangled from the corner of his mouth. It was horribly frayed at the tip, and it dripped into the grass. His chest swelled to its full capacity then sunk back in on itself. A deep and formidable whisper bellowed within his throat, and I sensed that it were an intelligible murmuring of great importance. How long had he been lying there in deathly silence, saving his remaining strength in order to utter this vital communication? Perhaps he could help me to comprehend his mortal condition. I placed my cheek near his lips, and listened.

His chest stopped moving, and it did not seem as though he were going to speak. It expanded once more, and an abundance of liquid shot out of his throat. It spattered upon my face, and ran into my mouth. I felt its vibration enter my being; my eyeballs began wobbling, and an eerie singing rang from the network of shadows strewn about the grass. My tongue felt as though it were consumed in flame. I tried to stand, but I became considerably dizzy, and rested my palms upon my kneecaps. The inscription on the sign had evolved into something entirely new. It read: *This field is impassable.* A great gust of wind swept through the field, and washed over my face. It set the many blades of grass to whispering and dancing. I spit the conflagrant fluid into the wind. It scattered into a faintly definable mist that sprayed across the sign. The sign began, again, to change. Its words formed into new, unrecognizable arrangements, but they did not move.

Earthquake?

Your town heaves
its thousand shoulders
and lets the china stagger

the yard seizes
up its collection
of roots

who patiently die
into the long
pores they left.

You feel now
you should have listened
to July and her quiet ideas

but you are so human.
You are most afraid
of familiar greatness

and cannot know that Earth's
precious shaking is nothing
but want to bloom.

Roommates

When the door opens, Jessie doesn't realize I'm sitting at the black dining room table, watching her. I don't think she even wonders why the light is on in our apartment this late at night. She stumbles on the hardwood floor, her heels clacking away like rapid fire. She steadies herself with the doorknob, walking like her ankles are chained together. Her blonde hair falls past her shoulders, obscuring her face as she pulls at the buckle straps of her shoes. The black dress has few curves to cling to and her stockings have a tear at her right shin. She's not used to wearing heels and when she plops them down by the door, she still walks like she's off balance. She sets her purse on the kitchen counter and it caves in on itself before falling over. By the glimmer of the dining room light, she locates the jar of peanut butter on the counter. It's new and she pierces the paper covering with her nails, tearing at it. A drawer rattles as she pulls it open, grabbing a spoon. She stabs the virgin jar and shovels a spoonful into her mouth.

"We wouldn't run out of peanut butter so fast if you stopped doing that."

She turns around when I speak, jar in one hand, spoon in her mouth. She pulls, but the spoon is a fighter and drags her tongue out with it. She does her best to get as much peanut butter off of the spoon as possible, but she soon withdraws her tongue to savor the overly sweet, sticky substance. "You don't like peanut butter anyway," she says after swallowing most of it.

"It's supposed to be for Becky's lunch," I say.

"She's already asleep?" She and I both know it's too late for Becky to be awake.

"I put her to bed already."

She's licking the spoon, trying to clean it as she watches me pretend to look at the printouts in front of me. "Why are you still up?"

"How was your date?"

I hear the spoon smack against her teeth and she pulls it away from her mouth. "It was fine," she says. "He's nice."

"Good for you, Jessie," I say, circling a phone number with my pen. All the papers in front of me rattle off details of various apartments and have pictures that are supposed to entice me. "Does he know about Becky?"

"He has a son, so he said that he understands," Jessie says, leaning against the counter. I can see her calves, tense through her nylon stockings. Her butt is too flat to stand out against her ill fitting dress that would slip down her if there weren't straps to keep it up. The fabric bunches around her waist, dragging it higher up her legs.

"Do you think he would be a good dad for Becky?"

She thrusts the spoon into the jar again, frowning. "No. He wanted to have sex in the car. Last time I did that, I got pregnant."

The next time Becky comes to me and asks where she came from, I wonder if I will have to tell her she was conceived in the backseat of a blue sedan because her mommy didn't have the heart to tell her boyfriend no. "He wanted to have sex on the second date? In his car?"

"I told him it couldn't happen in our apartment," Jessie says. "Is it strange for a guy to want to have sex on the second date?"

"I don't know. Probably." I go back to the apartments, trying to stare at them and not at her exposed shoulders.

"How come you haven't dated since we moved in together?" Jessie asks as she swirls the spoon around in the jar, her long nails scraping the rim.

"You're going to contaminate the entire thing with your spit," I tell her.

"You said we should start dating because having guys in our lives would be a good thing," she says, her voice rising. She's staring at me, still twirling the spoon in the peanut butter. "You said you wanted to get a boyfriend." I can see the front of her dress rise and fall back with her breaths.

"I haven't met anyone and it's kind of hard to get a guy," I argue.

"You're pretty enough."

"Jessie, I live here with you and your daughter. It's kind of hard to get a guy to date me the moment he finds out." I look down. One of the apartments is near two convenient shopping locations. How lovely.

"If you don't want me and Becky around, we'll leave," she says. "I've told you that a million times. If you're embarrassed, then just say it. I'm the one that's the single mother, not you."

"I'm going to get a promotion," I say as I get up from the table. The dim light from the dining room casts shadows on Jessie's face and she stops moving the spoon. She squeezes the jar and comes to the table. She's shorter than me, far more demure and feminine. Guys don't care that she's a single mother. They see her move to the backseat of their car, carefully pulling down her jeans while they fondle her. She has a shy sort of smile, with childish crooked teeth and when I look at her, I want to tuck her into bed just like I do Becky.

She looks at all the apartment papers, squeezing the jar until the plastic curls in, making sharp corners where the indents end. "Are you moving out?"

"Our lease will be up in a few months. I think we should move into a new apartment-"

"Three bedroom, two bath," she reads as she leans over the table. The dress exposes her spine and all its knobby contours. I want to lay my head against her back while running my hand over all of the ridges. She turns to look at me, her mouth open enough that I can see her tongue pressing against a canine.

"We should have separate rooms so we can actually bring guys home," I say. She's churning the spoon in the peanut butter and some of it is pushing up against the sides of the jar, piling up near the top. Her fingers are getting sticky, but she takes in such shuddering breaths that I hardly notice the mess. Her tongue pushes against the sides of her mouth, runs along her teeth, as if the peanut butter is still there.

She looks like an older version of Becky under the dining room light, except her eyes are piercing and she's wearing a short black dress that doesn't suit her bony frame at all.

"What about Becky?" she finally asks, her voice hoarse. "Whose room is she supposed to go to when she has a nightmare?"

"Yours. You're her mother-"

"But you're like her father."

She's leaning towards me now and my foot smacks the leg of the chair when I step back. She's breathing so hard that her chest might pop out of the dress or the seams will split and it will glide right off her, leaving her only in her underwear and torn nylon stockings. There's peanut butter all over the rim of the jar now as she continues thrash the spoon inside of it.

"But I'm a girl." My mouth is sticky and dry, my voice as tiny as Becky's when she's done something wrong. Jessie sets the jar down on the table, letting the spoon sink all the way into the peanut butter.

"It doesn't matter that you're a girl," she says. One of the straps of her dress slips down her shoulder. "I don't feel like dating if you're not going to date anyone."

She licks at her sticky fingers as she lays her head against my chest, letting her chin rest against her collar bone like she's a sleeping bird. She smells of peanuts and the flowery perfume I let her borrow. I wrap my arm around her waist and she moves closer to me, her ribcage expanding and contracting wildly. I'm waiting for the seams to burst, but they never do.

Deciding to Connect

An Essay

The candle is competing with dawn's dewy light through half closed curtains. I'm curled, collapsed sideways upon my bed, hypnotized by the possibilities painted across my laptop's screen. It sits above me, balanced on a headboard half its size, perched like a confident god, appraising me and my fate. It is the guardian of possibility. Dazed by the drunken courage that pushes me to press the keys, to respond with what I have been holding back for three months, three years, three lifetimes, I can't stop smiling, blushing, blundering through a moment made of wires and words. I'm a giggly schoolgirl. I'm in the afterglow of a night, nay two, of questions that keep coming compulsively and combatively. Mine and his, back and forth, creating a dancing game of insights the likes of which I've never lived before. We know more now than we did during the previous four years combined. Everything is open, everything could be. He presses me, pushes me into the center of the bush I was beating around for the last ten minutes. I say it, it's so silly, but it means more, "What would you do if I hit on you for real?" There is a silence that is deepened by the dead space in the text window, the flashing cursor line that screams, "Let there be more!" He answers me and stuns us both with a chick-flick level of irony. Four years. Four years he loved me, four years I held him on high, way up and well out of reach. I idolized him and worshipped at an altar turning to flesh before me now, melted by the heat of mutual confession. This is real. This is happening. We are real. We are happening.

We met writing online, in the distant days when I still did group writing daily, did it like the drug it is and was. They say you never stop being an addict, and it's true, but you can get busy enough to forget. I write for school, papers and essays and exams and academic reviews. Ideas are written by hand, jotted during class, framing color-coded notes with unrelated marginalia. Later I type; it's quicker, cleaner, and admittedly mandatory. Sometimes I read him my work, but usually I email it. I need second and third sets of eyes to review, to look for what I missed, for the mistakes that aren't allowed on the printed page. Mistakes always seem so much more pronounced once machine-measured ink and staples get involved. The night before it's due, I argue with my printer until it yields, and then methodically, I even out the paper, edge-to-edge, and pierce it, binding the pages in a definitive way, that at a glance, words alone could never do. But that act, that solitary stamp of metal jaws removes the freedom of a backspace bar or eraser. It's done, it's finished, and it can't be fixed. Sure, I could open the file and edit and print another copy. It's just a psychological block, not a tangible barrier; it's all in my head but then, so many of life's most powerful forces are.

I keep coming back to the flame and wax. The rosewood colored candle crowning my headboard, atop the cutout of the punk girl's pierced tongue (engraved with the words "SCHOOL BITES"). It's a conical candle, though the top was initially flat-ish—indented over time as fire and wick conspired against it. I think mom gave it to me three years before I ever used it. It had this strange marmoreal look to it, blending the rosy whole with pinkish-white swirls. I always remember it smelling like roses but I honestly don't know if it did. It's very possible my mind is melding the color with the content. It burnt out months ago, though I refuse to remove or really replace it, given the significance of the nights it lit. Now it is a solidified puddle of wax rung'round with dried rose petals in a wooden base: a beautiful grave for the overflow of all my other candles and the memories melted into each. I've played with wax since I was child and still can't have a lit candle around me without the temptation to toy with it. There's just something about how warm wax seduces the fingertips. Pliably pleasant without being messy, though it's easy to go there too: just dip a digit passed the candle's curled crest, down into the molten lake near its flame and bask in the brief burn that brands you with a second skin. But like the sensation, the smooth pink print is fleeting and peels off with undo ease, just another petal melting into the messier magmatic whole. Where does it really go? From cold and firm to hot and wet over and over again, does the same amount of mass remain, or does the flame's passion always take something away, something more than the braid it burns? Solid to liquid to gasping breaths of smoke, can a candle, collapsed and wickless, be considered dead, or is it merely waiting to melt again, revived by a lighter's princely kiss?

Hinged and metal, a stapler is two pieces that make one; even when bent back and opened up, its insides examined, the pieces stay together. An undervalued staple of the average desktop, it is often addressed with physical hostility, regardless of whether or not it works properly. It is spring loaded, but only decisive when enough pressure is applied. The pressured stapler offers an artificial link between two or more things, papery things. It pierces each and provides a suture to all, creating a new unit. Unlike the stapler, the new unit is one that can be readily undone, a fragile and temporary thing, yet even if the little metal staple is removed and discarded, the scar of its mark will remain, branding the pages with past intentions.

I scoffed at romance. It was a ridiculous fabrication of falsehoods and hypocrisy. I had only ever seen a handful of relationships that weren't drenched in the watered down residue of so-called love. Love: a word without meaning in the west. "Oh my god, I love that movie!" "Wow, I love your new haircut." "Ha! That's hilarious, I love you!" Is it any wonder I was so cynical? Every relationship I had ever been in left me scrambling for the escape hatch. I was a wolf, rabid for the hunt but skittering to halt when it concluded with that cage coming down around me, its bars forged of the words "Sure, I'll go out with you." All I wanted was to stalk prey, harry the heels, and maybe take a bite or two, but apparently such desires were mutually exclusive from monogamy. I didn't even like kissing. Some of high school's most monotonous memories are from the days before I gave up on dating altogether, the days when I sat in the backseat of the car with Johnny, making out and marveling at the wood of the garage. Back then, I ranked my disinterest by the number of random objects I counted while waiting for something to be over. In my childhood church it was windows and pews. During make-out sessions, I diversified: Bushes, garage panels, coins on the floor mats, songs on the radio, the lashes lining his closed blue eyes.

Is a stapler truly a unifier or is it just a temporary fix to a long term desire? Is the violence of its puncturing sexually symbolic? The staples the children begat from penetration, a parting from one whole into the other, tying objects together in a familial unit? Does the weakness of its used staples when contrasted with its own endurance denote the weakness of one when removed from many? Is a stapler merely an attempt to satisfy a need to repair humanity's inherent disassociation from one another, like different pages in the same story? Is the temporary fix enough to count? Are pages better for the mistaken marks they bear, the removed staples that make way for new work? Is the fragility and lack of permanence the point? Does importance come from how easily something can be undone, rather than how long it will last?

The wax crumbs are embedded in my bed sheets, hinting at the source of glazed drips. The stripped staples are strewn across my desk and a hundred sullied drafts. The candle corpse is coated in dust, like the stapler. We still sit with a screen between us most days, though breath-bound words come weekly as well. I write for academia and addiction. It has been sixteen months since a silly girl gained so much more from the forced courage that came with a silly question. More him, more us, more marks—punctures and burns and the loss of false skins—more openness, more awareness, more words, more questions. I can't count when I kiss now, but not because I close my eyes. There are still days when I'm a giddy schoolgirl and he's held on-high. There are also days when I drag him down to face an adult. There are days when we play with passions. There are days when we work to keep the connection. There are days when we don't stop writing until the dawn of the next. There are days when we still question, curled in the computer's light. And there are days when we don't need to ask to hear the answers.

Jah Works in the Rothko Chapel

Under the influence of blue, she sits in the chapel
and watches the walls painted in muted moods.

Above her, the misty rays of a shrouded sun
sift through skylights to kiss the purples awake
though she's more inured to the blacks and grays.

She is here today to think about why she loves you
when in the coming of her fantasies you feature
as prominently as a speed-bump.

She shuts her eyes and thinks instead about Jah
which to her feels unfamiliar, like slipping in
to someone else's something comfortable.

Still, it leads to a meditation on love
until her mind grasps the distance between
your slack romance and what she really needs.

Awake now, she looks at the landscape
of Rothko's painted dreams and blinks away the border
between thought and voice, longing to tell you

what you already know.

My Pal

There have been some strange things here, I tell you. Like the time my old buddy Billy had a pool party and suddenly there were sharks all in the water. Everybody was screamin and runnin around all nutso. Then, there was Mrs. Gluck, who had all those cats and when she died they died too! I heard stories that the smell in her house after she croaked, could make your hair turn white!

But 'spite that, 'spite dead cats and sharks, nothing beats my old friend RadioHead. He was old when I met him, already losing the sound out of the speaker in his face. Sometimes one of his knobs would drop off and I would pick it up for him. He was a funny old guy, the big radio, you know, like those old Telefunken ones with the big knobs and the big speaker, well that's RadioHead's face and it's perched on a pair of wiry thin shoulders that hunch perceptually. The old dude couldn't talk, maybe because he had a speaker for a mouth and all, but boy, could the music come out of his face. I like to "fellow" him around when he would come by with that long, loose gait ahis, all swingin his arms and the like. He gets this idea you see and all the kids hear soft music whirlin out of his head like angel's wings rubbin together toward heaven. I stole that line from a book, but you know what I mean.

Sos theres all these kids and the music and all and they just fellow him. Maybe they are playin baseball or war or you know playin at knock and run, but that music, its kinda like the ice cream truck comin down the block, with that little jingle and you've got your grubby hands in your pockets lookin for nickels, dimes and the best, quarters. It brings a smile to my face, thinkin about him, that music and before he's turnin the corner, I'm there to meet him. He keeps his head low, his shoulders hunched, maybe cause his Radio Head gotten a little too heavy in his old age. But there he is and I'm smili and he turns the knob on his face and a happy little song comes out.

I used to help him around, when he got the cane and he used to stumble a lot. I was one of the last that sees Radiohead around anymore, he's sittin out on his porch and he got a sad song comin out that speaker. He lost one of his knobs and I was at summer camp, so I couldn't find it for him. Those older boys know he's old and play jokes on him. These boys got cars and radios in their cars and they got music that they can play for themselves and who needs a dumb old Radiohead anyway? But I like him and I take care of him. We sit on his porch and watch the sun drop under the earth and he plays them sad, wistful, songs and sometimes I get up real close to hear them and maybe I can't. But I am dreamin of the sky and that music and of angels playin up in heaven. It's Radiohead and me and it's alright.

Idiots Abroad

christ
you hear that accent behind you
and it reduces you to nothing

sitting in a small café
trying to shove down lunch
with all of that vatican wealth
gleaming gold in the distance

you hear that accent

dull and american
slow and purposeful

like john wayne hungry
for a ham and cheese sandwich

and it just lowers you into the dirt

in fact, none of them are even trying
to speak the language
or even read what's on the menu

they just demand and demand again

talking louder as if it will make a difference
in the translation

but this has been par for the course

idiots abroad in the eternal city

wearing their baseball hats
and football team t-shirts

taking the piss out of the italians
with their boorishness

photographing everything in sight
but taking in nothing

chanting usa! usa! when the mood hits them

packs of these well-heeled yanks
roaming around with that clueless american gaze
their ignorance buffered by
single file tour groups at the pantheon
and a sense of global entitlement

pulling along their angry kids

the trust fund daughters on high school vacation
complaining about not being at the mall

their young asses getting fat on gelato

the thick-necked sons laughing
at the penises on priceless sculptures

trying to pick up italian girls
with nothing but that foolish and taxing
american swagger

jerking each other off in hot hotel rooms
with not enough air conditioning

you hear that bland, self-righteous accent behind you
and it reduces you to rubble

takes you out piece by piece

because you are a part of it too
this red white and blue abomination

although you try to hide your shame beneath
the veneer of thoughtfulness and quiet

of polite discussion
and a bit of banter over the house wine

you are an idiot just as well
through no fault of your own

and that waiter smiling nervously at you
as he cautiously pours out the red
into two crystal glasses

chalices that catch the last orange glow of the sun

well, he was just dressed down by a tableful
of your countrymen
dressed in bright old navy t-shirts
and grand canyon hats

for the cardinal sin
of not having decaf coffee on the menu

and now he's just waiting on you
for whatever it is that'll make you strike.

Wreckers

A ribbon of blood stole across the horizon as the first of the wreckers stepped out of the grove onto the sand. They scratched out craters in the dunes for the pine knots. The wind swept the smoke down the beach toward the inlet.

The sky was slate gray, and though the rain had stopped the wind continued to whip all along the beach. When the boat had failed to arrive as scheduled, the telegraph office had wired every office along the coastline. Word had spread quickly.

For a time, the lights from the listing boat could still be seen from the tops of the dunes. She had come a thousand miles across the sea, only to sink fewer than a hundred miles from harbor. Foundering on a shifting bar, she took on water and sank, the lights in the berths sizzling in the salt water as the boat slipped under the waves.

Ashore the gray lumps lay along the beach for two hundred yards. Tossed upon the sand at high tide, they lay half buried already.

Their skirts had dragged them under. They had been only a few hundred yards from shore when the boat went under. Any closer and they could have touched bottom, walking in to the beach and down the road to the hotel, where they would have been given dry clothes and cups of steaming coffee; bottles would have been uncorked for them, though it was only dawn.

Along the edge of the water in the predawn darkness, a figure prowled among the dead. The only sound the wind.

He brushed the blue crabs away from a face as he knelt over a drowned girl. Her lips were blue, and her dress flapped in the wind that had not let up. He studied her calves, pale and flattened where they lay splayed upon the sand.

He wrenched a silver bangle from the girl's wrist. The arm flopped back onto the damp sand. He tried but could not slip a gold ring from her finger; the water had filled up the body, and though he dragged her a full five feet it would not pull loose.

Later, when the first of the wreckers arrived, pine smudges flickering in the wind, they covered the bodies with sheets. Logs and chunks of driftwood were rolled over the corners to keep the cloths from blowing away. Sand flies settled on the sheets. There were hundreds of them; they covered everything.

The unsocketed finger lay yards away from the rest of the girl, uncovered by the sheets. Even if the wreckers had noticed the mangled hand as they carted the body to the sandy plot that had been dug out in the cemetery, there would have been no reason for anyone to waste time searching for half a finger lost in the sand.

By noontime, the tide had drawn the finger back out to sea, where it drifted in the current, pointing back across the sea to the old world.

The Clock

Some nights I see faces

blinking at me in the dark—

robin's blue eyes,

heart-shaped lips,

pink gums.

It always happens afterwards,

when we are rubber soft,

our mouths full of nothings,

when we rock together

like a lullaby.

Last night could be Billy,

and tonight could be Samantha,

and this could be our bed

with the lumpy mattress;

this could be our house

with the creaky stairs.

When you roll me over
I won't think of them—
their hands clasped around my neck,
little baby sighs crying
their little baby cries.

Instead I soothe you to sleep
and we dream into Saturdays.
Soon we will walk out
of a rented house
in search of milk and biscuits and eggs,
The Sun, and a kiss goodbye,
and coffee.

Deer Hunting

"Come on, Roger." I call back but don't turn my head. That guy's always behind. Has a belly and can't keep up.

"Gotta lay off those beers, Rog," says Cormac. He's beside me and hanging onto his rifle like it was his old lady.

I slow as we approach the glade and Cormac slows too. "Watsa matter, Rog, too much sex last night?" I say this but I doubt he's getting any. "Could you keep up then?"

Cormac's tiring too, wants to get home to his wife. These guys have a lot of personal stuff they're hauling around. I keep moving forward but glance over my shoulder and see Cormac stop on the trail we've been following, then duck between some overgrowth and push his back against a tree.

"Naw," says Cormac. "Too much sex for him means his arm's sore the next morning."

"Better be careful Rog," I say over my shoulder but keeping my voice low now. "You won't be able to squeeze the trigger."

The trail stops ahead where blue starts to show between the trees. I know he's in there. When we spotted him from the ridge he was going that way. There'll be a creek in there plus it's getting dark. He thinks he's gonna spend the night here.

I drop flat near where the glade opens, and kind of slide along, then get sick of that and crawl on my knees, the wood on my rifle warm in my hands and my elbows getting roughed up through my shirt from the sticks and stuff under me.

Suddenly my face has sun on it and I don't even have to search around for him. He's standing right in the middle of the goddam glade. Huge antlers. And he sees me. I don't bother staying on the ground looking stupid. I get up, slow like, and lift my rifle the same way. He's looking at me kind of stupid, like he got caught with his pants down.

He can't run, he probably knows that. If he does I'll shoot him in the rear and it'll be a goddam mess trying to track him and his blood through the bush so I don't want to take too long. I don't call the guys. They're messing around on the goddam trail. I look at those dark pupils. They're like creatures themselves and they glitter like a kids sparkler. That's what life looks like right there. All sparks and a calm wildness. Holding a rifle at a creature's head gives a certain insight sometimes. Except, I know it's the dimming light filtering through trees that's glimmering around in that deep wetness. I look at the nose, soft –looking, breathing. This guy knows something I probably should. Whatever it is, it's not doing him much good.

I'm happy as hell. 'Course I am, I should be, I'm ready to squeeze off a good shot. I think: God did a lot better job here than he did on those idiots back on the trail. That conjures them up maybe, 'cause suddenly there's sound from the bush.

"Where the hell are you," says Roger. I swing around so quick that before I realize, I've got my crosshairs between his eyes; white saucers flying around like they'd spin off into the brush. He's barely lifting those poor sorry legs, so when he sees me they buckle and he crashes into the clearing. I think: maybe God knows what he's up to some of the time. I lower the barrel and turn around while Roger starts up cussing. Darkening shadows settle in an empty clearing.

I turn back and set an arm on Roger's shoulder. "Where the hell's Cormac?"

Tennessee

The clouds coming. The color shift in the sky, the dark impression they leave behind, cutting out space. I want to go somewhere like Tennessee where there's two "n's" and two "s's" and two "e's". Where old men beat off twice in a row on their balconies -- stubs of cigars nailed in their teeth, big red noses, pores like crates. And they laugh, laugh loudly while rocking, rocking on their grandmother's chairs – wood like old bones. The sun goes down everyday: Same time, same place. And their eyes turn up to look.

The Other Way

For Jane Williams

Dalen Way was fired for sticking his cock in the container of mozzarella. There was no mystery about it and it wasn't kept under anyone's hat – the yelling from the manager's office in the back was enough for those who hadn't stood witness to the scandal. They all saw Dalen shuffle out on a Tuesday afternoon, with his hat in his back pocket and as he turned at the door to throw his nametag to the sidewalk, the remaining employees of The Sauce Shack saw something in his black-black eyes, something that said, 'You'll see me again.'

But they never did.

The replacement for Dalen Way as a delivery boy was chosen by the usual method. Mr. Hamilton, who had been manager for the past two years, collected old pepperoni sticks from around the shop – under an oven, behind the register, in the employee restroom – and held them out to his flock of young sheep. Each one, looking warily at their co-workers, reached out and chose.

When James pulled back the shortest, most shriveled excuse for a pepperoni stick he'd ever seen, the others cheered. Their sticks were cast to the floor, they rolled and scattered under various pieces of furniture until they were needed again someday, when yet another delivery boy was lost to the shuffle, the tizzy, the desperation and bleakness of their way of life.

James looked down at his pepperoni stick, green eyes narrowed.

He was sure that was what drove Dalen Way to stick his cock in the mozzarella. James was just a lowly pizza chef but he had heard the horror stories – the delivery boys on the curb in front of the shop, swapping stories about low tips, no tips, someone once given a penny and some lint if they hadn't been satisfactory. No longer was James assured his meager restitution nor the safe warm womb of the shop. He was thrown to the wolves, those wild things in hovels way out there, those things they call delivery customers. And all because... all because-

"Of this pepperoni," he murmured, voice choked.

A meaty hand clasped his shoulder suddenly and the pepperoni stick dropped from James' hand. He watched it roll away, awaiting the next rapture under some secret place.

"James! Glad to see it's you who'll be replacing Dalen," said Mr. Hamilton, whose bright red face was smiling. *Smiling.* James wanted to reach out and smack it. "You'll do much better than that delinquent, I think."

More than anything, James wanted to protest. This didn't seem like chance to him. It was damnation. Over Mr. Hamilton's shoulder, he could see through the glass doors of the shop and the two boys who stood on the curb, smoke rising from their open mouths and the cigarettes between their fingers. He thought of how depraved it all was and glanced back at Mr. Hamilton.

Please, he wanted to say. *Please, send Jessica or Wayne or Michelle. Or even yourself; God knows you could use getting out a bit.*

But when he opened his mouth, a burp came forth.

Mr. Hamilton laughed heartily. "That a boy! You'll fit in out there just fine!"

The next day, James came to work with the taste of ashes in his mouth. The drive to the shop had been a horror, filled with the heat of June, the blare of lunch-hour honking and rage, the music blasting from open windows of cars all around him, the stop lights grinning in his face like Mr. Hamilton.

He realized, nearly comatose in the driver's seat that he would endure this all day. Every day. Forever and ever, until death released him or insanity broke him.

As he pulled into the parking lot, he saw his fellow delivery boys, Ethan and Brandon, standing against a concrete pillar which held up The Sauce Shack. They looked at James who sat there in his car, feeling sorry for himself, and in their gaze was something knowing and – perhaps – warm. James left the safety of his car and went to them.

Their hair was plastered to their foreheads and cheeks by way of sweat. Their cigarettes were centimeters long and the two ends together looked at James like monster eyes, angry and red.

"Want?" Brandon pulled out a pack of Marlboros and held it openly to James.

James looked at the little sticks and exhaled. "No thank you…"

"Aw," Ethan simpered. "Cheer up, dude. You shouldn't look like such a lost cause, especially if you're going out to see customers. Best foot forward."

James looked down at himself, his red shirt, his black pants with the stain he could never get out. "Do I really look like a lost cause?" he asked.

"A sack of sad," Ethan said.

Brandon nodded in agreement.

"I just don't want to be here," James muttered.

"Shows," Brandon said, sticking a second cigarette into his mouth beside the dying first. James opened his mouth to respond but the door behind them opened – the blast of AC at James' back reminded him of safety and love. Mr. Hamilton called out in cheerful tones that there was a delivery ready to go out and he looked to each boy, wondering who would answer that hell's bell.

He waited for his fellow delivery boys to spare him this one time. He wasn't ready, he felt sick, he felt hot, he needed a drink of water and a nap. He looked at them with pleading eyes.

Best go get it over with, Ethan had said to James before handing him the pizzas and addresses. Back in the scream of the sunny afternoon, James decided maybe they hadn't looked at him with warmth and understanding at all, but maybe with recognition and relief – here was fresh meat to take some of the heat off of them.

James felt like a fool.

He felt that way as he pulled to a crooked halt in some beat-up parking lot of dilapidated apartment buildings. His head ached from the glare of the sun on the pavement and windows and his stomach growled loudly, encouraged by the sweet smells of pizza. James eyed the two boxes he carried into the breezeway of one building and knew they probably wouldn't be as satisfying as pizzas he'd made himself.

Yes, surely the future of The Sauce Shack was in grave peril. The quality of pizza which their customers all over town had come to know and, yes, even depend upon to feed their withering children would plummet. Angry calls. Protests. James could see it all as he approached apartment F12. Rioting in the street, rotten tomatoes hurled at Mr. Hamilton's house in the suburbs. Soon, he would have to reinstate James in the kitchen – the lives of everyone depended upon it.

It was only a matter of time.

He knocked and the lurch of motion that followed nearly caused him to drop the two pizzas he carried. The door opened like a hurricane was behind it but he looked down to find a woman, her shoulders only coming up to the doorknob and the face atop them was like the aftermath of Katrina, framed by orange hair. But she looked at him with brown eyes that were at first soft with adoration and then hardened to disdain.

"Dalen?" she asked.

James bit his lip. "Um, no, sorry. He's not working at The Sauce Shack anymore."

She stared.

James waited a few seconds and then cleared his throat, reading the receipt in his hand: "I have a double-cheese-"

The door slammed shut and James let out a bleat of surprise, stumbling a foot back and balancing the pizzas in his left hand. He called out to the woman on the other side of the door, asking her if she could come out, please, because her pizzas would surely become cold and this wasn't very fair to make him drive out all that way and then just slam the door in his face which was rude, by the way, and won't she please come out or at least crack the door so they could exchange the boxes and the money.

The door didn't budge and after ten minutes, James walked away.

When James arrived back at The Sauce Shack, battle-weary and downtrodden, he lurched out into what was now nighttime the way that woman had before lurched out at him. He held her order in his thin arms, the pizza now cold and brittle. After the other orders he had delivered – all successful despite his meager gain in tips – he felt hollow, like an empty pizza box.

Ethan was there to greet him and although James resented his earlier casting out into the cruel world with little ceremony, he went to Ethan as a work-weary husband would go to his wife.

"Terrible," James sighed, coming to stand with his co-worker on the sidewalk.

Ethan paid him little mind as he snatched the pizza boxes from him. He peered inside. "Anchovy? Who really eats anchovies?"

"Some crazy woman who didn't want her pizza."

"Oh." Ethan picked up a slice and shoveled it down. As he started work on his second, he eyed James who'd slid down the cement pillar to sit on the sidewalk. "So, she didn't want them, eh? What's wrong, did she hear about how our guys have a tendency to stick their cocks in product or something?"

James frowned out at the street, the rapid lights flashing, the music that ran in a constant hum. "I don't know. She came to the door saying Dalen's name, so... maybe. She slammed it on me when she realized I wasn't him, though."

There was a pause in the obscene lip-smacking from above and James glanced up to find Ethan grinning down at him.

"What?"

"You got one of his old customers then!"

"Was he so popular?" James' mouth twitched to a pout. "I didn't know him, but he seemed kind of… well. Like a jerk." *Like the rest of you delivery guys*, he added internally.

Ethan suckled cheese from the tip of his fourth slice. "Nah, you've got him all wrong. Dalen was one hell of a charitable soul."

"He was?"

"Yeah! Couldn't you tell? I mean, what'd the chick look like?"

James recalled that moment when her face appeared before him – it was like a knot in a tree not far up from the ground. He remembered looking at her and longing to look away but fearing for his tip if he balked. The realization now that he hadn't gotten a tip despite his friendly service made him bitter.

"She looked like a short horror story," he grumbled into his arms.

Ethan nodded sagely. "Sounds like Dalen. Bet you he fucked her good too, like you'd do a model. She's probably hurting over his leaving; you shouldn't be too sour over it, man. Maybe she'll tip next time." He moved his pierced tongue around in his mouth and finally spit something out – it landed on James' car hood.

"You mean to say he… that he-"

"Of course!"

"So…"

"Just think of it, man. A hot pizza and a hot cock, delivered in less than thirty minutes or half off your next buy! Sounds like one hell of a promotional, doesn't it?"

James rarely had nightmares. He rarely remembered his dreams – that is, if he did indeed dream at all – but when he woke up the next morning, covered in sweat and panting, he remembered vaguely him sticking his cock into the vat of mozzarella. Everyone stood around him watching, the delivery guys, Mr. Hamilton, the pizza chefs, and they stood expressionless and placid, as if this was always where he would end up.

When he looked down into the vat, it wasn't mozzarella at all but that short woman's mouth engulfing him like a black hole, she who was an eternal downward spiral into madness.

James was now sure that she was what had driven Dalen Way to the mozzarella vat. She was nothing compared to meager wages – James imagined himself in the dream again, being connected with her in that way. He couldn't bare it. The image made him cringe, twitch, shudder all the way to work.

Brandon and Ethan were gone by the time James arrived – they were out amongst the people, hustling, and perhaps even fucking. Ethan never said it was an uncommon thing Dalen did. Perhaps it was normal, just a part of the delivery life. He wasn't sure what to think.

It all sounded a bit like a bad pornography, he thought, but even then it was a thousand times worse. At least bad pornography had sexy women.

Mr. Hamilton greeted him with a frown and a mouthful. "Ethan told me about your debacle last night! You can't just go alienating our customers, returning here with orders undelivered. Do you want to sully the company name? I know you don't, James, you're a good kid. But damn, this kind of thing just can't continue. Sure, it was just one customer but she's been extremely loyal! We can't lose our loyal customers, James. You know what loyalty means in this business? Everything, that's what! Now, here, you take this personal pan pizza and skedaddle on over there. This is free to our jilted customer. Tell her you're sorry for any infraction. And do us all a favor and lay it on thick."

James had the personal pan pizza shoved into his arms and was whirled around by Mr. Hamilton's meaty hands. He met the day nearly in tears.

F12. He saw the apartment number in front of him and knocked, ready for the lurch.

There was none.

He knocked again, louder and more forceful, he was tired of the summer swelter and the few hornets that buzzed lazily in the breezeway. As he ducked one, he heard a timid call from inside: "Come in."

He recalled that same voice that had trembled and asked, *Dalen?*

But come in? Just walk in? James shifted on the concrete and held the hot pizza in his arms. He debated leaving it in front of the door but Mr. Hamilton would surely have a problem with that. He felt like the man's face was over his shoulder - watching, judging, urging him to go inside and…

… *and lay it on thick.*

James turned the doorknob and the apartment was opened to him, the air conditioning pulling him into the living room, the door closing behind him.

"Excuse me," James called, treading onto the carpeted area. "This is a free…"

She came from the darkened hallway, into the living room where light from the glass patio door fell on them both. Her hair was frizzed as it had been yesterday and it seemed like she hadn't changed clothes. Bags drooped under her brown eyes, those same eyes that had looked at her with apprehension and now placidity.

"I knew you'd come back," she said.

James imagined her and Dalen but soon shook the image from his mind – too much, too much to bear. "This is a free personal pan pizza from The Sauce Shack. Please accept this as penance for my offence yesterday and my failure to deliver your order." He held it out to her.

She walked across the cream-colored carpet as if wading through water. Her stature reminded James of a child in the shallows, one walking out into the deep. Her small hand extended, she touched the heated box and said, "You know my name from the order yesterday, don't you?"

He nodded, trying to put the pizza in her hand. "Rebecca," he muttered.

She moved her fingertips back. "You're Dalen's replacement. Aren't you?"

"Yes," James said reflexively. Then he looked into her eyes and said, "No, I mean, not like *that*, I… I just deliver pizzas and… well."

Rebecca looked at him and James felt something akin to guilt. But he couldn't. He looked at her and couldn't. He looked at the couch – some plaid lump in the room that smelled of chicken gravy – and imagined Dalen delivering to her there. He felt his breathing become labored and he shoved the pizza at her, turned on his heel and ran.

Tips were lax. James returned to The Sauce Shack at the end of the day after six deliveries and had two dollars in change jingling in his back pocket. He found Ethan leaning up against the cement pillar again and came to him, eyelids heavy, patience thin.

"This sucks," he said. "I'm not making any money and my days are nothing but disappointment. I might as well not work at all."

Ethan raised an eyebrow. "Well, join the club! You expect me to feel sorry for you when I'm in the same boat? I went out twice today and-"

"Only twice?"

"-and I made like fifty dollars. It's getting harder and harder to afford new and stylish rings." He stuck his pierced tongue out for emphasis and James noticed the bright red ring.

"I've been out six times and made two dollars," James said, staring at the ring with malice.

Ethan retracted his tongue. "Well, obviously, there's something wrong with your service."

"There's nothing wrong with my service! I'm quite friendly to everyone."

"Friendly doesn't always do it – are you putting your ass into it?"

"My *ass*?"

"Maybe you ought to switch positions more often. Or less! You know, I could help you better if you had a video to show me."

James felt the color drain from his face. He looked up at Ethan's calm expression and couldn't tell if he was joking or not. "You mean," he croaked, "you too? *You too?*"

"I too what?"

"You have sex with your customers?"

"… you don't?"

And lay it on thick.

James eyed Mr. Hamilton warily, wondering if he knew what his delivery boys were up to. Or maybe it was all a giant trick, played by Ethan. He could imagine Ethan confiding in Brandon at the end of the day, cackling, *Oh, guess what I told James today? That we all fuck our customers, that Dalen did it too, that it's all just a big push for tips! He believed it too! Oh, you should have seen his face. Ha. Ha. Ha.*

James couldn't stand the thought of it. But he didn't know who to ask for confirmation – Dalen had walked into the sunset that one fateful day, never to be seen again. And Mr. Hamilton would possibly toss James out after Dalen if he were to ask such a thing and be mistaken.

So the idea came to him when Mr. Hamilton said, "There's a delivery!" and Rebecca's name was on the ticket.

He never thought he would rush to that place – thirty minute policy be damned – that rotten, dilapidated complex and the dank hole in the wall that was apartment F12. Way out there in the sun. James raced through streetlights, cars honking, bums on the side of the road, holding signs that said: WILL WORK FOR MONEY.

James wondered off-handedly, *But how hard would you work?*

He arrived there, went lurching towards the door with her order in one hand – some cheese and anchovy-covered concoction a lesser chef had thrown together. When he knocked, he felt every emotion he'd had since receiving his shriveled pepperoni stick.

She opened the door.

"What is it I'm supposed to give you here?" he cried out in a voice much like that of a helpless toddler. "What is it you're looking for?"

"Dalen," she said.

"Well I can't give you Dalen," James said desperately. "I'm not him. I don't have him. I don't know where he's gone."

"Then you'll have to do." And she said it with a horrifically solemn expression, one which did absolutely nothing to help her look more attractive. A pink frock draped her small body and James saw the outline of a potbelly and pert nipples calling to him. Her eyes, brown and empty like holes into sewage systems, begged. She begged. She looked at him and begged. Her demeanor was desperation and loss but she stood there with purpose, all of her four foot five stature. When she opened her mouth, her voice seemed far away and she said, "You're not so bad looking."

It was probably a compliment. James remembered that sign he saw on the way over.

WILL WORK FOR MONEY.

How hard are you willing to work?

He followed her inside.

The last time James had sex, he was in his childhood bedroom in his parents' house, just a few months before high school graduation. He remembered the familiar smells of his blankets, the comforting glances around the room at his book shelves, his aurora borealis posters, his guitars. And it was because of such things that the newness the girl brought to the room – her scent of plumeria, her cries like kittens mewling, her tugging at him – wasn't so bad; in fact, it was almost enjoyable.

Now, here.

Here in apartment F12, way out in the broil of the city night, the walls surrounding him, the kipper scent of Rebecca, her cries that sounded like a dying walrus, her thrashing beneath him like a tuna pulled from sea.

James watched the clock that ticked above her headboard. He tried to keep thoughts of how this state was only temporary - of how, soon, he would be speeding from this place with money in his back pocket, with F12 behind him. But for some reason, the clock couldn't keep his attention and he glanced downward and he glanced downward into a black hole.

James drifted back to The Sauce Shack in a daze. His head ached and his legs were heavy. He felt some kind of absentness in his groin as if his cock had receded from pure shock and horror. Misuse? But there was nothing he could do about it. He lurched from the car and found Brandon and Ethan there on the concrete, both looking at him with similar expressions.

James shook his head vaguely and began to fall. He was caught by strong arms and looked up into Brandon's stony face. Ethan appeared at their sides and he was trilling, "Paisan! Paisan!"

So.

They could smell it on him, then. James closed his eyes and felt the muscle beneath the cotton of Brandon's shirt. Was it Rebecca's scent still clinging to him, like the scent of shit lingering long after using a public restroom? Or was it that wad of money in his back pocket, no longer the metallic jingle of coins but folding, life-giving, beautiful bills?

Or was it something else entirely?

A week went by and James found his stride. He fell into step with his fellow delivery boys and stood on the concrete between orders and accepted cigarettes from Brandon and spoke to Ethan about getting a tongue piercing. He looked up at the blood orange sky in the evening and waited for the ticket that said *Rebecca* in hard black and white.

It was a doom-call, it was a hell's bells ringing, it was the swing of the scythe and no one but James answered it. He knew what waited for him in F12. It was his cross to bear. He would not give it to Ethan or Brandon – he was Dalen's replacement and with that mantle of delivery boy came everything that Dalen had once held: his swagger, his tips, his customers. Rebecca. He inherited Rebecca.

Tip worries were a thing of the past. James had answered his own question. How hard was he willing to work?

However hard the customer wanted.

He marveled sometimes at how many lonely people there were. Before, when he was just a lowly pizza chef, sheltered in the warm tomato-scented womb of The Sauce Shack, he had not known. He had not seen the city for what it was – the people that surrounded him, all so needy, all so *starved*. James brought them nourishment.

And oh, he'd seen *women*. Beautiful women, women who answered their doors in negligees, women who answered their doors in nothing but pearls, women who read the nametag on his uniform and whispered his name to him in the heat of their moment. He'd seen the insides of upper-middle-class homes, he'd seen soirees and little black dresses. He'd felt their gazes creep up his back, slide down his stomach to rest at his belt. He was a drop of blood in the ocean where sharks hunted. He was a pizza delivery man in the night.

But no matter where he roamed, who he fucked, how fat his wallet became, he always found himself back at F12.

He was sucked into that black hole again and again. His inheritance.

One night when he was sitting on the edge of her bed, his pants around his ankles, the clock ticking away the seconds of his life, she said, "You're not like him at all."

It was the first thing she'd said to him since, *You're not so bad looking.* That had been a week ago.

James turned to look at her, laying there like a starfish on the ocean floor. She was pink and bared to the ceiling. She looked at anything but him and James felt something akin to anger rise up in him.

Not like Dalen?

He *was* Dalen as far as the world was concerned. Customers, co-workers, even Mr. Hamilton sometimes called him *Day*. He was the fucking *sun* since he'd gotten the hang of being a deliverer. Customers raved. He carried the shop on his back. And had there really ever been any doubt that it would come to this? He was a great delivery boy, just as he had been a great pizza chef.

He remembered Dalen's swagger as he walked out of the shop. He remembered wondering back then what would become of them all.

Here he was on Rebecca's bed, giving her everything Dalen had and she had the nerve to complain.

"What, then?" James snapped. "What is it you want from me? What did he do that I don't?"

"He loved me."

She said it simply and without fear of laughter or scorn. Something deep inside James felt moved but that which was surrounding it could think it was nothing but delusion. A delivery boy turned whore turned lover? How many things was he expected to be? How many things could Dalen Way have *been*?

But this was too far.

"How do you know?" James asked. "How do you know he loved you?"

She said nothing, only looked up at the ceiling.

"Admit it. You don't know that. None of this has any basis in reality. You wanted pizza so he brought it. You wanted someone to fuck you so he did. He gave you what you wanted and you mistook it for love. You believed someone cared. But we don't come here to care. We come here to deliver pizza!"

"You're nothing like him," she said and laughed. She laughed and the sound, oh, like wedding bells on a cool spring morning. Cherry blossoms and perfume. Her laugh echoed in the room, in the apartment, in James' head. It was a force that pushed him from the bed, propelled him to the door. He took a look at her, laying naked and laughing, as free as a petal on the wind.

He looked down at his uniform.

When James arrived at The Sauce Shack, his legs shaking and his face red, he looked up at the building under the yellow moon and wondered if, so long ago when it was Dalen Way here in this spot, when it was Dalen Way there in Rebecca, did he ever think of those who came before him?

There had to be those who came before.

Had to be.

Dozens, hundreds, thousands of pizza boys who walked in and out of this shop - those who came before even Ethan and Brandon, who James strolled by on the sidewalk in front of the shop. He knew he must've looked a sight – eyes ringed red, brown hair mussed, limbs in tremors.

"James," Ethan said but James was deaf.

Brandon touched his arm but James was numb.

James opened the door and the cool AC wrapped him up and he saw the pizza chefs mulling about behind the counter. They didn't notice him and for a moment, he felt himself again: who he really was beneath the tips and the delivery and the uniform, these bondages that had been slapped on him one by one, these bondages that he had no way of resisting.

He remembered mulling about like them under the florescent lighting with that comforting scent of tomato and pepperoni surrounding him. His eyes were set on his task but really, they'd been closed. He hadn't seen a ray of light until Dalen Way opened the door that day, strolling out.

He remembered the look on Dalen's face.

How then must James have looked as he jumped behind the counter? How then must the pizza chefs have seen him when he bent to grab a shriveled old pepperoni stick from under one of the ovens? Mr. Hamilton stood by, his red face round and jiggling as he said something to James, as James wandered over to the vat of mozzarella cheese.

He imagined that someday they would see him again. He imagined how he'd tell his tale and how they'd applaud him and tell him he'd done Dalen proud. But they'd say that he hadn't gone crazy like Dalen. They'd say he kept himself. They'd remember the day when he looked down and laughed as he plunged the pepperoni into the cheese.

Pretty Much It

She told him she saw a housepainter the other day wearing white coveralls, and how he had paint drippings on him and splatters of every color under the sun. How he was like a walking work of art.

They were on the fire escape, drinking tequila straight from the bottle. And he was watching a flock of pigeons circle one of the tenements, where a man with a bamboo pole with a red rag at the end of it was churning the sky, seeming almost magically, to be influencing their flight.

Art is where you find it, he told her. *Butchers wear white too. But red on white is pretty much it. Another kind of art, I suppose.*

Pork chops were on sale the other day, she said, after a long silence, taking the end of her dress and fanning her thighs with it.

He tossed the empty bottle over the wrought iron bars and listened to it crash five stories below. There was Puerto Rican music coming from one of the open windows and a couple in their underwear, in a blue-walled room, dancing to it.

Pork chops are good, he told her.

The Face of Cosmology

I didn't think it was possible for plastic trees to drop their leaves, but it's happening at Ted's house. There's a little pile of green plastic leaves around the base of a plant that looks like a small fig tree. I ask him about it. He says it's a work of nature and he doesn't question it. How can it be nature, I ask, when it's plastic? Very simple—physics, he says.

Ted has been talking physics and cosmology to me for months now. If we aren't fucking, then he's into explaining the cosmos to me. I don't know that much about the universe, but I have Googled some of what he says, and I can tell he doesn't know that much either. It sounds good—all those beautiful words about black holes, bosons, quarks, and charms. And he can string all that stuff together like a mad man on too much caffeine. I like to listen to him and watch his enthusiasm, his eyes wide, his hands shaping small objects, the excitement in his voice about *what this all means*. That's the part I'm most interested in, but we don't ever seem to get there. It's like he sort of partly explains, and then it's all *a mystery*.

I agree with that. It's been a mystery for a long time, and every now and then, some scientists come up with a good guess, an educated guess as Ted calls it, and for awhile, that's truth. And then it's not. And then it starts all over again. There was a time when I cared about figuring all this out, but now I don't. It's kind of like a game or a math quiz in which you never can find the answer, and it's sort of like religion because you accept the parts you like and toss out the parts you don't, and the rest is *all a mystery*.

So when I kind of gave up trying to figure out the universe, I turned most of my attention to fucking and to food. Right now, I am eating baby back ribs with a honey barbecue sauce while Ted tells me the latest on the cosmos and how this suggests a God, but not really. It's the not really part that gets to me, but I know asking about that will draw us into an endless conversation, maybe a quarrel, and, besides, I would rather eat. So I am wiping honey barbecue sauce off my mouth with those tiny napkins from packets they give you with take-out orders that are never large enough even to wipe your lips with, let alone your hands, and Ted is winding down. This is the point where even he's tired of talking about all this, and he reaches for a beer. He likes to show off by opening the bottle cap by twisting it with his fist. He always gets the cap off, but sometimes the edges cut into his fingers and make them bleed. This is one of those times.

Damn it, he says. He's rinsing his hand off at the sink and starting into some stuff about the nature of water and how if you add in an extra hydrogen molecule you have hydrogen peroxide, and how'd you like to drink that?

I wouldn't, I say. And he turns around and looks at me and says, What?

Then I realize he's not that interested in what I think or even if I'm listening. Mostly he's talking to himself, a kind of built-in audience for his own ideas. And I wonder why I never realized this before. Maybe because I really wasn't listening all that much either. At a certain point, you've heard it all, and it becomes repetition. You really do get to know people, at least in the sense of what to expect from them. And so the idea that you can be with someone and continue to discover new things about them seems bogus to me. But you're supposed to do that, to be on some sort of journey of endless discovery when you are with someone. And I guess it's true in a way because I have just discovered something about Ted and about me. For him, I'm like wallpaper—there, but not really necessary. And he's like TV for me, something to watch, but often with the Mute on, while I do other things that interest me more, like eating.

I'm almost done with the ribs. Ted has one hand wrapped in a paper towel and the other holding his beer. He takes a sip, stares at me, and seems puzzled. Maybe he thinks it's odd I wouldn't want to drink hydrogen peroxide, or maybe he thinks it's weird I would interrupt his thoughts with a comment of my own. Maybe he's had some kind of discovery of his own about me and about himself. I don't know. I'm not sure I care that much. We don't talk about much except the universe, and I am getting really bored with that subject. Last night, Ted told me he wanted to be the face of cosmology, go on TV and explain it all to people, and become famous for that. I had a hard time visualizing that because I don't know how many people would tune in for that or how long they would listen to him, as he does tend to go on and on. I suggested maybe he could make a YouTube video and see how many views he got, and determine from that how famous he might become, but he blew me off on that one.

I finish my ribs, and Ted finishes his beer at just about the same time. I know he will burp, and he does. Then he smiles at me. We are going to fuck, which is okay by me, and much better than some talk on the physics of sound that he usually gives me after one of his burps. So it's, C'mere, baby—and I do. I'll give it to him that he has a nice embrace and a pretty good kiss. I like the way his body feels against mine, and that will do, for me, in place of big answers about the meaning of life and what the heck we all are doing here, floating around on some piece of rock in what appears to be infinite space.

So I let him lead me into the bedroom, to the bed, and to the way we both undress each other. And then he kisses me, and I can feel him breathing hard. I'm pretty sure he bought those plastic leaves at Wal-Mart the other day and put them under the plastic fig tree, probably to get to me to ask about it so that he could do one of his talks, which really is a monologue. But that's okay. If he wants to live in a world in which he thinks I am dumb enough or trusting enough to believe that plastic leaves drop from plastic trees, I can live with it. I just wonder if he can live like that, or why he would want to. And I realize he has never given me one of his talks on fucking, or eating, or anything else we do together. Maybe I really am just wallpaper to him, just there to watch the show. So I let him have at it, the kind of fucking he likes to do, and I realize that we both are part of the cosmos that is fucking at this moment, all over the globe and maybe out into other planets and galaxies somewhere in infinite space. And I'm okay with that. It's cosmology the way I understand it, and I'm sure that Ted would, too, if he really gave a damn.

Truth or Dare

Small doses of strychnine

can be used to cure paralysis.

So can large doses of aspirin and wine.

Displacement of weight on a bed of nails

prevents internal injury.

As can be witnessed by the resting heart rate.

There's enough creation to go around.

What is lost can only be found

in the last place searched.

The worst parts of ourselves

are mirrored in those closest to us.

Spontaneous human combustion

renders the body to ash

yet leaves the surroundings untouched.

Things don't own you.

They can't take you with them.

Stars are only children who strayed off

into dark rooms carrying candles.

There are more dark rooms than candles.

Every confession is just a forgiveness

you have to feel your way around.

As can be witnessed

in the soft breast of a lover

and the hand that leads you there.

Seven Miles

Bird never waited for me to make it into the house. He always sped away as soon as I shut the door to his rusted 1989 Beretta with a maroon hood that didn't match the rest of its dark blue body. I always wished he would stay—just for that one extra minute—just in case the door was locked—but he never did. Dropping his sister's best friend off after a sleepover was far too much of a burden on a Sunday morning.

Today the door was locked. Of course it was. With Ma and the Big T disappearing for days at a time and big bruv spending most nights at his friend's house to avoid the bugs, there was no one left to let me in. If one of our eight cats was smarter they might have been able to. But they were cats. To think a cat could unlock a deadbolt's just plain ignorant—even as a young child I knew that.

It was winter out. Chill breezes of spring slept away the current season. Summer hung in the rafters, out of sight. All was quiet and still save for Bones nya-ing in the window closest to the front door. Of all the cats he was my favorite. He always kept me company when I couldn't get in.

Why did I not have a key? Good question. Ask Ma. Though you won't get a cohesive answer. She'll likely ramble on about how God has a mission for her or how the leaves of the trees clap as she passes them by—or her book, the pages upon pages of nonsensical gibberish where she depicted herself as the next prophet.

I sat on the porch for a while. There was this old rocking chair with a worn-out back that fit my ten-year-old body perfectly. I sunk into it just enough to be comfortable, but not enough to get stuck. Bones nya-ed and I rocked. Around us the gentle flakes of January blanketed the Orchard.

After an hour—or what I thought was an hour—my fingers and toes begged me to get inside. The front door to our three-bedroom apartment filled with cats and bugs had an opening for a window at its top. The glass of the window had long since been broken by some drunken incident. It had been replaced by two thick pieces of cardboard. If I could break through the cardboard there was a chance of reaching in to unlock the door from inside. I blew heat on my fingers and began to pry.

This didn't work. My hands were too small and useless to do any good. They did nothing more than rip tiny pieces of paper facing off the makeshift window. Eventually they grew too cold and sore for any more trying. It was obvious that another plan was in order.

At the time Ma was married to her third husband, the Big T. 'T' stood for Tony or Tom or Terrence, I can't recall. They were only married for six weeks before she got the annulment—not long enough for me to form a concrete memory of the guy.

The Big T had a house in Ludlow, around 3.5 miles away. I figured that, if they weren't home, they might be there. Where else could they be? As I couldn't get in to the apartment I knew that walking to his house was the only solid way to get warm.

So I walked. I said my good-byes to Bones and I made my way down the un-sanded porch steps. The snow was several inches high at the bottom, causing me to wade through it. The wind picked up as I headed down Main Street. It scratched my face the way Bones did one time when I pulled his tail a little too hard.

Down the road the apartment renters actually shoveled their sidewalks, making it easier to move. My legs carried on a little easier and my pace quickened. So did the wind.

Passing the Grand Theatre, I thought about warming up by watching a movie—it was only a dollar back then—but the Grand was a small theatre. It played only one movie at a time. Today's movie was R rated. I couldn't have been able to get in without a note of permission from my mother. If I had paper I could have forged a note,

Ma's signature was a few squiggly lines masquerading as her name. All the paper was in the house, though, so I kept walking.

The Orchard Variety came up a while later. I bought a cup of hot cocoa. They wouldn't let me drink it in the store so I had to take it with me, but that was okay. I had something to warm my hands and that was all that mattered.

Crossing the Ludlow Bridge was harry as it was slippery and there was no pedestrian walkway. Doing my best to hug the very edge of the bridge's frozen metal rail, I cried as the cars sloppily drove by, fishtailing this way and that. They honked at me and shouted for me to get out of the road. Not one of them stopped to ask me—the little girl crying alone in a blizzard—if I was okay.

When I made it over the bridge and into Ludlow I stopped crying. What remnants of tears I did have clung to my cheeks like icy balusters. That's when I began to think this was a bad idea. If I'd only stayed on the porch and waited it would have shielded me from the ice and the increasingly scraping wind.

But I couldn't go back, not now. I was closer to the Big T's house than I was to our apartment. It didn't make sense to turn around. No, the only way out of this was to press forward. With renewed drive I marched on.

Eventually the cocoa became as cold as the rest of me. I was so thirsty by then that I downed the entire contents of the Styrofoam cup, despite the increased chill that crept upon my insides. The sugar did help, though. It provided a little more energy to fuel my tired legs.

Finally, finally I reached the street where the Big T's house resided. I'd made it... I'd made it! Dear God, I had made it. More excited than I'd ever been, I ran toward his beige L-ranch, the sixth one down on the left hand side.

Relieved, I walked up the front steps and knocked on the door. No response. Maybe they were asleep? I knocked harder. Still nothing. I rang the doorbell in rapid succession—the only response I received was the sound of the *ding, ding, ding* echoing off the hallway's burnt orange walls.

It can't be. They have to be here, they just have to! Maybe if I go around and knock on the back door they'll hear me better. It's worth a shot...

Knocking on the back door yielded no results. The house was empty. They were not home. I remember so clearly how I felt when I realized that no one was there—like a coat hook caught mid-way inside my chest every time I took a breath.

For the second time that day I cried—I wailed, actually. Above the sound of the whipping wind I doubt anyone heard me. I still wonder if someone did hear me and chose to ignore my pleas for help—given my experience on the bridge I figure it's likely.

The trip back was so much worse than the trip forward. By that time my hands and feet were so cold it felt like a thousand tiny needles were pricking them over and over. Crying as loud as I could I hoped a car would stop and help me back home—the notion of not getting into cars with strangers was not my top priority.

No one stopped. An F150 did hit a puddle, drenching me in slush. The iced water slapped my face and trickled underneath my red winter coat. I wailed louder. The only response was the wind wailing back.

Crossing the bridge for the second time was the same as crossing it the first. Cars honked, people shouted, I hugged the barrier. I wouldn't understand what a terrible place the Orchard was for many years. When I finally realized that it was filled with nasty, uncaring people, I'd long since moved and their selfishness could no longer touch me—well, it does, sometimes, but I do my best to ignore it.

My only dollar had been spent on the hot cocoa. As I could not afford another, I had to bypass the Orchard Variety. That wasn't such a big deal. By then I was less than twenty minutes to home. My cries subsided. They were pointless now. I'd be back on my porch very soon.

I was not thirty-feet from home when the cop car pulled up beside me. The officer leaned over and opened the door, motioning for me to get in. It didn't matter how close to home I was. The car was warm, no doubt. I climbed in without a second thought.

He asked me if I was okay, what I was doing out in the storm and where it was that I lived. I knew if I made a big deal out of it I'd catch hell from Ma, so I lied. I told him I'd walked down the street to buy a cup of hot cocoa. The officer asked me where the cocoa was. I lied and said I'd finished it in the store.

A light was on when we arrived at the apartment building. Bruv must have been home. Eagerly I threw open the car door and ran up the steps, taking them two at a time. So what if I fell? I was covered in winter, anyway.

The officer followed me into the apartment, obviously unconvinced by my story. Bruv was on the other side to greet us. When he saw us he looked ashamed, both from keeping me locked out and the squalor in which we lived. It was easy to see how disgusted the officer was by the living room. He did little to hide it. After telling bruv to get me into a hot bath he left us there. Social Services would arrive several days later, but that's a different story.

I was frozen, inside and out. Looking back I know I was close to frostbitten. At the time bruv knew, but he didn't know what to do about it. The best remedy he could think of was a boiling hot bath, so he started one. I undressed and climbed into it. My fingers and toes burned so bad that I wanted to rip them off. Bruv told me to stay in the bath as long as possible, that I needed to 'thaw out.' After five minutes I could no longer take it. I got out, threw on some mismatched pajamas and crawled underneath as many blankets as we both could find.

In retrospect I was lucky that no permanent damage had been done—no physical damage, that is. I could have come out of that experience with lost toes or fingers, but I didn't. The only thing I lost that day was what little faith I had left in my mother.

Ma didn't come home that night—or the night after that. When she finally did show up smelling of Black Mambo and weed, I'd gotten over the walk and everything that came with it. I couldn't have mentioned it to her, anyway. Ma did no wrong. To tell her about the walk was to insinuate that she'd done wrong by not being home to let me in. To insinuate that she was wrong was to face her rotten side—the side that was even more rotten than was typical. I didn't want to deal with that again.

Bruv and I never told her what happened. To this day I doubt she knows. It's better that way, I think—just one less reason for her to have one of her fits. She did have a fit when Social Services showed up, but luckily she blamed it on her sister. Colleen had called them several times before, after all.

People wonder why I stopped speaking with my mother so long ago. They don't understand. They call me callous and cold. Some see me as the monster, not her. That's fine. Perhaps I am a monster. Perhaps I am callous and cold. But to my critics I have this to say: If I ever have a daughter, I will never, ever make her walk seven miles in the snow.

AUTHORS

Marie Abate
Marie Abate is a poet and writer. She has an M.A. in Writing from Johns Hopkins University. Her poetry has recently appeared or is forthcoming in *Weave; The Sewanee Theological Review; In Posse Review; Free State Review; SF&D; Smile, Hon, You're in Baltimore;* and *The Mom Egg,* among other publications. A recent *Best of the Net* poetry award winner and *Pushcart Prize* nominee, she lives and works in Baltimore, Maryland.

L. Alexandra
L. Alexandra is a communications tutor of eclectic interests, who recently decided to pursue a Creative Writing degree. Her work first appeared in the 2012 issues of *Obscura* and *Claro* under the name L.A. Smith. She was later published on *Vox Poetica* and has another piece upcoming in the 2013 Spring edition of *Obscura*. For her, writing is a compulsion as well as a calling (hence, the necessity of the four notebooks she keeps perpetually at hand). Influenced by Nabokov, Flaubert, and Angela Carter, she views figurative language as one of the most powerful tools at a writer's disposal and often pairs it with repetition and alliteration to give her work a musical quality. While L. Alexandra started in fiction, favoring fantasy, she has since written academic essays, nonfiction, poetry, blogs, and flash fiction. Outside of writing, she spends her days talking in excess, over indulging in stories in their many forms, and clinging to the delusion that she will be able to remain in school forever.

Audrey Allen
Audrey Allen is a writer living in Los Angeles. Her experience includes working as a journalist for newspapers such as the *Santa Monica Daily Press* and *The Outlook*. She studied fine art at Art Center College of Design, and danced classical ballet professionally, touring with Nevada Ballet Theater in 1995.

Rachel Berger
Rachel Berger is in the process of earning her MA in Creative Writing at the University of Hull. When not in class or wrestling with her novel, she tries to spend as much time traveling as she can, dipping her toes into travel writing. She made her published debut in *Crack the Spine*.

Donavon Davidson

Donavon's poems have appeared, or are soon to appear, in: *Moria, Identity Theory, ditch, FRiGG, The Rusty Nail, Thirteen Myna Birds, Eunoia Review, The Legendary, Spork, Softblow, decomP, Barnstorm, The Fiddleback, Prick of the Spindle, Juked, Pirene's Fountain, The Montucky Review, 3:AM, Anti-, Pedestal, WordRiot, MiPOesias, Stirring, Evergreen Review, Barnwoo,* and many others. He received his MFA from Goddard College and currently teaches writing at the Community College of Vermont.

Colin Dodds

Colin Dodds grew up in Massachusetts and completed his education in New York City. He's the author of several novels, including "The Last Bad Job", which the late Norman Mailer touted as showing "something that very few writers have; a species of inner talent that owes very little to other people." Dodds' screenplay, "Refreshment – A Tragedy," was named a semi-finalist in 2010 *American Zoetrope Contest.* His poetry has appeared in more than sixty publications, and has been nominated for the *Pushcart Prize.* He lives in Brooklyn, New York, with his wife Samantha.

Molly Fuller

Molly Fuller has studied at and received degrees from Ohio University and Sarah Lawrence College. Her work has been published or is forthcoming in *Hot Metal Bridge, Quickly, Crack the Spine, Potomac* and the Cutty Wren Press broadside series. Her chapbook, "The Neighborhood Psycho Dreams of Love" is forthcoming from *Cutty Wren Press.*

Adam J. Galanski

Adam J. Galanski is an emerging writer and punk rock musician from New England living in Chicago, Illinois. Currently he attends the Fiction Writing program at Columbia College. He has worked in tattoo shops, supermarket delis, inspecting oil tanks and delivering Chinese food and has previously been published in *Crack the Spine, The Manila Envelope, Horror Sleaze Trash, Underground Voices E-Zine, Drunken Absurdity* and more.

Janae Green

Janae Green is a recipient of the 2nd Annual *Gypsy Sachet Awards in Letters and Biography* from *Fiction Fix.* Her poems and short stories have appeared in *Atticus Review*, *Eunoia Review*, *Fiction Fix*, *Paper Darts*, *Poetry Quarterly*, *scissors and spackle*, *The Ofi Press* and various other online and print literary journals. She lives in the Pacific Northwest with her partner, artist Shea Bordo.

John Grochalski
John Grochalski is the author of "The Noose Doesn't Get Any Looser," "Glass City," and the forthcoming novel, "The Librarian." He lives in Brooklyn, New York.

Srother K. Hall
Strother K. Hall is a native of Powell County, Ky., and currently lives in Georgetown, Ky. He spent several years as a newspaper reporter and editor. He has several incomplete projects floating around and thinks it's about time to start knocking them out again. His first book, "Lost Change and Loose Cousins," a collection of stories with Aaron Saylor, will be published in Spring 2013 by *Point Nine Publishing*.

Christina Harrington
Christina Harrington is an MFA candidate at Sarah Lawrence College. She is also the editor and founder of *The Abecedary Project*, a print-only literary magazine dedicated to rare and under-used words.

Max Henderson
Max Henderson is a doctoral student in physics at Drexel University. Originally from Coatesville, Pennsylvania, he researches neural networks and quantum computation when he's not too busy watching Adventure Time. His poems are about making mistakes while drinking a good, dark beer. He has been published in *Black Heart Magazine*, *Crack the Spine* and *Citizen Brooklyn*.

Brian Hobbs
Brian Hobbs loves writing and finds if he can write a poem, a story, or a witty rejoinder once a day, he has his soul bread. He has recently been published in *Milk Sugar*, *Yorick*, and *Scissors and Spackle*. His day job is his second love, teaching. He hopes to be a writing Voltron of Delilo, O'Connor, and Frucht.

Chelsea Johnson

Chelsea is a soon-to-be graduate English major from Azusa Pacific University. She will be attending Eastern Washington University in the fall for a Master in Fine Arts degree, emphasizing in fiction. Until *Crack the Spine*, she was previously unpublished. Chelsea is working on completing her short fiction collection and dabbles in the world of non-fiction and editorial journalism. She enjoys poetry that isn't about love, Harry Potter, and is convinced that one day she will become a Jedi Master. Her spare time is spent petting her cat and acquiring useless information — for example, a ragamuffin is a type of cat.

Dini Karasik

Dini Karasik is a Mexican-American writer and lawyer. Her work has appeared or is forthcoming in *Crack the Spine*, *The Más Tequila Review*, *Red Savina Review*, *Zombie Logic Review*, *Kweli Journal*, and *Bartleby Snopes*. She is currently writing her first novel.

Jane Rosenberg LaForge

Jane Rosenberg LaForge is the author of the full-length poetry collection, "With Apologies to Mick Jagger, Other Gods, and All Women" (*The Aldrich Press 2012*); and three chapbooks. Her most recent chapbook, "The Navigation of Loss," was one of three winners of the *Red Ochre Lit* 2012 chapbook contest. Her experimental fantasy novel and memoir, "An Unsuitable Princess: A True Fantasy/A Fantastical Memoir," will be published *by Jaded Ibis Press* in 2014.

Randi Lee

Forever inspired, Randi Lee can often be found scribbling notes on the backs of napkins and Chinese-food receipts. Over the years these scribbles have evolved into many published stories and poems. Writing short, creative pieces is Randi's specialty—however, she recently began writing her first full-length novel. She hopes to publish this novel soon and is already working on its sequel.

Chad Lowther

Chad Lowther is a poet from Ohio. He currently lives with his wife in Albany, NY, where he is working toward an M. A. in English and an M.S. in Information Studies at the State University of New York at Albany. He also serves as co-editor of *Brarzakh Magazine*, a poetics e-journal, run by the University's English Department. He has read his work with the *deepcleveland poets*, and the *Albany Poets*, as well as at the *Omega Institute* in Rhinebeck, NY, in Manhattan at the *Bowery Poetry Club*, *CBGB's*, and the *Sidewalk Café*, and at countless coffee shops and bars throughout the U.S.

Jennifer Mayo

A soon to be graduate from the University of Colorado Denver, Jennifer Mayo is majoring in English Creative Writing with a minor in Communication. She works as a student fiction editor for the *Copper Nickel*. In her spare time, Jennifer practices the Japanese sword martial art Iaido, plays too many video games, and also enjoys sampling baked goods made by friends.

Steven Minchin

Steven has spent the past three years confused, believing he was an asteroid. Once back on Earth, a trip which mearly required him to lift his head, he found himself again crashing hard in New York's capital city. There he found his mistakes, murmurs and travels appearing in *Four and Twenty*, *mad swirl*, *Short, Fast and Deadly*, *vox poetica*, and *Heavy Hands Ink*. Steven continues, unless he's dead, at which point he will not. He plans, at that point, to switch from continuing to silently cohabitating in an omnipresent way.

Christina Murphy

Christina Murphy's stories have appeared in a range of journals and anthologies, including *A cappella Zoo*, *PANK*, *Word Riot*, and *Spilling Ink Review*. Her fiction has twice been nominated for a *Pushcart Prize* and was the winner of the 2011 *Andre Dubus Award* for Short Fiction.

Maury Nicely

Maury Nicely lives in Chattanooga, Tennessee. His work has previously appeared in *Prick of the Spindle* and *Clapboard House*.

Linda Niehoff

Linda Niehoff is a photographer living in a small Kansas town. Her work has appeared in *Literary Orphans*, *Scissors & Spackle* and *Circa Review*. She's been a finalist in *Glimmer Train's Very Short Fiction Award* and Short Story Award for New Writers.

Olyn Ozbick

Olyn Ozbick's stories are published in *Monkeybicycle*, *Underground Voices Print Anthology*, *Fourthirtythree (4'33")*, *splinterswerve*, *Crack the Spine*, and other fine places.

Krista Ramsay

Krista Ramsay holds an MFA in Creative Writing from Butler University, where she served as Poetry Editor for *Booth: A Journal*. Her work has appeared in issue fifty-one of *Crack the Spine*, on *vox poetica*, and is forthcoming in the Summer 2013 edition of *Inclement Poetry Magazine*. She is an avid musician and homebrew enthusiast, currently residing in Indianapolis, Indiana, with her husband, Dave, two turtles, Gary and Otis, and a rabbit, Buliwyf.

Robyn Ritchie

Robyn Ritchie is a student who gets by on a lot of coffee and a little writing. She's been writing about men for years and still has little if any understanding of them.

Robert Scotellaro

Robert Scotellaro has published short fiction and poetry in numerous print and online journals and anthologies. He is the author of five literary chapbooks. His most recent collections are "Rhapsody of Fallen Objects" (*Flutter Press*, 2010) and "The Night Sings A Cappella" (*Big Table Publishing*, 2011). A full length collection of his flash fiction, "Measuring the Distance" (*Blue Light Press*, 2012), was a finalist for *The Eric Hoffer Award*. He is the recipient of *Zone 3's* Rainmaker Award in Poetry, and the author of three books for children. Raised in Manhattan, he currently lives in San Francisco with his wife and daughter.

Samuel Snoek-Brown

Samuel Snoek-Brown teaches and writes in Portland, OR. He also works as production editor for *Jersey Devil Press*. His work has appeared in *Bartleby Snopes*, *Ampersand Review*, *Fiction Circus*, *Red Fez*, and others, and is forthcoming in *Eunoia Review* and *SOL: English Writing in Mexico*.

Karina van Berkum

Karina is from small town New Hampshire and now lives in Baltimore, MD where she asks and answers questions. She's not sure she's lived enough to have a bio yet, so consider this one happily "in progress." She loves writing about seasons and the body, and her poems have been published in several literary magazines including *Stirring,* and *Vine Leaves Poetry.*

Haden Verble
Haden Verble has had several stories published in the past two years. This one, "Cold Water on Blood," is one of three set in Greenville, Kentucky. The two other Greenville stories can be found in the Arkansas Review.

Michael Welch
Michael Welch is a graduate of the Pacific University Writing Program. His recent publications include "Whatever Helps Gravity" in *Stealing Time*, "Equal to Fertility" in *Forge,* and "Letters from the Front", an essay about his work in Folsom Prison, in *The Mankind Project Reader.* "Torso, Front and Back" is upcoming *Prime Mincer,* "In Real Life" in *Foxing Quarterly,* , and "New Room" in Monkey Puzzle Press's *The Savage Consortium.* He grew up in the South Bronx and now lives with his family in Eugene, OR.

Visit www.crackthespine.com to subscribe to our weekly digital magazine or to review our submission guidelines.